About the Author

S.K. Benz always wanted to write stories. Writing and creating a world that can be a joy to whoever reads it is her passion. This is her second book and is pure magic. *God's Game* came from the heart and was perfect the first time it was written. She thanks all the sources that helped her write this book. She wishes the readers and the whole world a blessed and abundant life.

Gods' Game

S.K. Benz

Gods' Game

Olympia Publishers
London

www.olympiapublishers.com
OLYMPIA PAPERBACK EDITION

Copyright © S.K. Benz 2023

The right of S.K. Benz to be identified as author of
this work has been asserted in accordance with sections 77 and 78 of
the Copyright, Designs and Patents Act 1988.

All Rights Reserved

No reproduction, copy or transmission of this publication
may be made without written permission.
No paragraph of this publication may be reproduced,
copied or transmitted save with the written permission of the publisher,
or in accordance with the provisions
of the Copyright Act 1956 (as amended).

Any person who commits any unauthorised act in relation to
this publication may be liable to criminal
prosecution and civil claims for damage.

A CIP catalogue record for this title is
available from the British Library.

ISBN: 978-1-80439-113-6

This is a work of fiction.
Names, characters, places and incidents originate from the writer's
imagination. Any resemblance to actual persons, living or dead, is
purely coincidental.

First Published in 2023

Olympia Publishers
Tallis House
2 Tallis Street
London
EC4Y 0AB

Printed in Great Britain

Dedication

I dedicate this book to love, joy, and happiness.

Acknowledgements

Thank you to my mother, father, sisters, Harpreet and Aman, dear brother, Harbir, and my uncle, Manjeet Singh Bains. They all helped me write this book, and they don't even know it. Thank you all.

Two love birds were flying higher and higher in the sky. They were, so much in love that they forgot their surroundings and just kept enjoying each other's company. They kept looking at each other lovingly and were not sure how much time had passed before they got to a tree. It was a big tree and it's broad branches, green, lemon-scented leaves, and blackberries made it quite heavenly.

The two birds sat in the tree, oblivious to the surroundings. They were unaware that sitting there in the tree were Magical Love, Ms Destiny, The Evil of Hate, and Mr Fate.

Magical Love looked at the two birds and could not stop admiring their love, saying, "This is what I talk about; this is true love. When two people are in love, they see, eat and breathe only love. I am so powerful that it blinds people, and they only see love in each other. No wonder love is the most vital power in the whole world."

Ms Destiny was sitting next to Magical Love and nodded in agreement. However, she added, "I agree with you, Magical Love. Love is the strongest emotion, but I am the most powerful because if people choose not to chase love, they don't attain it. People need to strive and put in the effort to fall in love. Nothing comes by itself or without serious thought, and I do not help people unless they are committed to something."

Mr Fate could not stop himself from interfering and said, "I hear a lot about blind love and life choices. Yes, love might be the strongest emotion, and destiny might be the most powerful force, but I am the truth. I am the truth of this life. The truth is that you are born with a fate, and that is what you get, no matter what you do or don't do."

Ms Destiny just shook her head in disbelief and said, "If that is true, what is the point of life? What is the point when one person works to make the future better and others do not? If we are born with a fixed fate, then I should not exist."

"No, you should not," said Mr Fate. He smiled and looked at The Evil of Hate, who was sitting quietly for now, as if to ask for his input.

The Evil of Hate grinned and said, "You are all missing the point. I can make these two lovebirds kill each other in a matter of seconds. That is how hate works. No matter how much you love each other, a moment of hate can end it all. A moment of hate is all you need to finish years of love, affection and good relations. I know you might disagree with me, but that is what we see every day, and not only in the land of Aliesalba, but also in the land of Wellingtonia . It might not be as prevalent there as in Aliesalba, though."

No one said anything, for The Evil of Hate had a valid point.

As they kept quiet, The God of all Humanity came along and joined them. He looked at them all and asked what the issue was.

Ms Destiny said, "We are having a hard time deciding who runs the two worlds that we own. Each of us consider ourselves the strongest; however, The Evil of Hate made a valid point that hate is predominant everywhere, no matter whether it is the land of Aliesalba or the land of Wellingtonia."

The God of all Humanity thought for a while. He looked at them, then looked at the two lovebirds, who were just happy in the moment. Then he said. "Who wins or loses—destiny, fate, love or hate—depends on only one thing: the willpower of the person to whom you are applying your powers."

"These two lovebirds are under the power of love now, and if any other force was applied to them, they both would react differently, according to how much willpower they have."

"Who gives them this power?" challenged The Evil of Hate.

"I do," said The God of Humanity, smiling. "I give willpower to all of my humanity. How much they use it, I leave to them. I want everyone to have equal opportunities in life, regardless of where they were born and work or how they are clothed."

At that, all the other gods laughed.

Mr Fate looked at The God of Humanity and said, "Equal opportunities? How could you even say that, let alone make someone believe in that? Aliesalba is the land of no opportunities. If I simplify it—people are mostly short of money, don't have much work, wear anything available, and enjoyment can only be found in what they do every day, like daily chores. You are being political when you say that you provide equal opportunities to everyone. Do you think that we believe you when we know that the land of Wellingtonia is rich and prosperous? People are happy and know how to enjoy life, and to give you more perspective—they have started getting people from the land of Aliesalba to work for them." Mr Fate looked at The Evil of Hate as if to say, 'Equal opportunity? That's the biggest joke one can tell.'

"I don't want to say anything..." said The God of Humanity.

And before he could finish his sentence, Magical Love spoke. "You have nothing to say against this, respected god. I have also seen that people fall in love more when they are happy and have everything and, most importantly, if they have time. These birds are free and have no restrictions, so they can love. However, it does not matter which land we are talking about. People these days do not fall in love, and if they do, they keep it hidden as if it is a weapon of mass destruction."

The God of Humanity sighed and again started speaking, but

before he could finish his sentence, Ms Destiny said, "I agree with The God of Love. In the past, a person who fell in love would do anything to change the course of their fate to get the destiny they wanted; however, these days, it is very rare."

The God of Humanity took a deep breath and started again by saying, "Even if I say something, none of you will believe me."

Then The Evil of Hate, laughing, interjected, "You want us to believe you? I have not even said anything, and your own gods are contradicting your statement on equal opportunities. If anyone provides equal opportunity, then it is me. I give equal opportunities to hate; no matter whether people are rich or poor, if they hate each other strongly enough, the consequences are the same, such as not talking to each other or pushing each other or, in extreme cases, just killing each other. None of this has anything to do with wealth. I should be The Evil of Humanity, and you, The God of Humanity, should be hated."

The God of Humanity looked at all of them as if to ask them to say anything else they wanted to; however, they all kept quiet this time.

So The God of Humanity started, "Rather than saying anything more on this topic, I would like to have us compete, and, thus, we can figure out who is the strongest. That will also make it clear that I do provide all of them with equal opportunities, although none of you agrees."

"Well, you can show us what you would like to show us," said the Evil of Hate. "However, it seems like a bet to me. If you lose, what do we get?"

"I will give my crown to whoever wins out of all of you." In turn, he looked at Magical Love, The Evil of Hate, Mr Fate and Ms Destiny.

"What are the rules?" asked Magical Love, who loved to play fair.

"What is the show, though?" asked The Evil of Hate. "That is more important to know than the rules." The Evil of Hate had never cared about rules in his life; thus, he knew that even if there were rules, he would find a way to break them.

"The show is that we will take life from these lovebirds."

Everyone looked at The God of Humanity in surprise.

"Let me finish this time before any of you say anything," he continued. "Once dead, they will be reborn in a place agreed upon by us. Then the bet is on whether they can not only make it back to each other but also fall in love. And if they do, then will they allow themselves to be together or not?"

"That is interesting," said Mr Fate. "What would their fate be, though?" Mr Fate wanted to make sure he won, as did everyone else.

"You get to decide that, for you are fate itself," said The God of Humanity.

"Hmm," said The Evil of Hate. "I like it. Separate them so much so that meeting is impossible, let alone attaining love, and I do have a great idea for that. One of them will be reborn in Aliesalba and the other in Wellingtonia, and not only that, one will be born to a family with nothing and the other to a family with everything."

"I would suggest the male be born in Aliesalba and the female bird in Wellingtonia," said Ms Destiny.

"Oh, so you do want to win and make it easy for you? You know that a male has more chance of changing the course of his life than a woman," said Mr Fate with a smile. "If anything, it should be the other way around. We want to make it as difficult as possible for them to have a fair go."

Ms Destiny did not like Mr Fate's suggestion and asked, "So what do you think their fates should be?"

"The lady's fate, as with all other women in Aliesalba, is to give birth and be nothing. The man, however, as with any other Wellingtonia man, can attain the highest rank possible in the land of Wellingtonia. He will be, in fact, the Prince of Wellingtonia."

"That does not seem fair to me," said Magical Love. "How on earth would they meet each other, let alone fall in love and find a way to be together? It would not be possible."

"Well, if we want to make it difficult—and that is the first rule of the game—we should make it so difficult that it is almost impossible," said The Hate of Evil.

"Then it is too easy for Mr Fate and The Evil of Hate to win," said Ms Destiny, looking at The God of Humanity, who was just listening and looking at the lovebirds as they enjoyed themselves without any consideration of any other presence.

However, he did hear the question asked by Ms Destiny and said, "I know you don't believe me, but don't you even believe yourself? If fate had that much power, then he would be ruling the world, and to win, you only have to defeat Mr Fate, not all of us."

Ms Destiny did not reply.

"What are the rules?" asked Magical Love. "Who wants a fair go?"

Together, they devised the following rules:

There shall be fair play. Do not interfere physically; watch till the end.

1. A win or loss is not decided while both or one of the lovebirds are still fighting for love. We only conclude when both of them accept their fates and what life offers to them.

2. We are allowed to awaken them and make them realise the powers that we have given them; whether they listen and use the power is up to them.

3. We talk to each other about any issues.

4. Most importantly, none of us will harm either of the lovebirds.

The God of Humanity looked at everyone for any questions.

"What will the winner get?" asked the Evil of Hate.

"The winner is accepted as the strongest by all of us," said The God of Humanity.

"What about the loser?" asked The Evil of Hate

"I only want to have a winner, not a loser," said The God of Humanity.

"It seems to me that you have already accepted your defeat. There have to be consequences for the loser or what is the point? And we agreed on almost everything, and you contradicted what we said, so unless you win, you'll be the loser, The God of Humanity, and if that happens, then you are giving away your crown, and your humanity, and will be hated by everyone. There will be no more humanity in this world."

The God of Humanity thought for a while. *If I lose, the whole of humanity loses. It does not seem fair.*

"You are taking a very long time," probed The Evil again. "If you change your mind now, then you have to accept your defeat and the consequences will be the same."

The God of Humanity had no option but to say yes.

"So, the only way you win is if they both attain love, and become one like they are now; anything less than that will be your defeat," said The Evil of Hate, as if very sure of The God of Humanity's defeat and wanted the rules to be clear and precise.

The God of Humanity agreed, and both birds' lives were taken, and they were reborn again, the female lovebird on the land of Aliesalba, short of money and also work, and the male lovebird on the land of Wellingtonia, rich and prosperous.

Mr Fate made sure to choose the girl's family, one that had nothing but never-ending struggles to survive.

The boy had everything. He was born as a royal and had all the love and support in the world.

Now that the stage was set, the show started, and all the gods left to explore the earth and agreed to meet after seventeen years, for by then, the kids would be at a point to decide if they wanted to choose fate or go and explore destiny.

So the show started.

The male lovebird was born as the Prince of Wellingtonia named Prince Deutzo Hydrang by Queen Mother, who lived with King Father, her sister and her sister's husband. Wellingtonia was happy, rich, and prosperous. Prince Deutzo seemingly had a bright future until this point, visible to any eye; thus, no gods give much attention, and the main attraction was the female lovebird.

The female lovebird was born into a struggling family and had two sisters. The girl's father named the girl Phloxia, for he thought she looked different to everyone else in the family. "Little Phloxia looks like a flower," he would say, and they all adored her beauty.

Mr Fate had chosen this family for Phloxia for only one reason, and that reason was so he could have an easy win. The family was impoverished. The father did not work, for he was an alcoholic. The mother somehow made ends meet, but the only thing visible to Mr Fate with his peepers was the tension between the family members and the lack of peace in the household.

Still, it was not Mr Fate's fault that this was all he saw. It was the visible truth to an onlooker, and Mr Fate could only see with two eyes, and beyond that, he could not because he never wanted to and never needed to, for most people were living lives that he approved of. 'A life that involved no challenge and acceptance of what came their way.' However, with Phloxia, two things were against him. Firstly, every other god wanted to win, so they had given Phloxia as much of their powers as they could. Secondly, Mr Fate wanted to win as soon as possible and decided to provide her with close attention as she was growing up, but the closer you look the lesser you see. Thus, he could always see what Phloxia was doing in a particular moment but never could see what her intentions were for life. In contrast, the other gods had decided to wait seventeen years.

Phloxia's family was not how it looked from the outside. On the inside, it was a very different picture. The family was called the D. Dron family because of their intelligence and high status in society, as 'Dron' means 'a great teacher'. The great-grandparents had worked as educators and had property and other assets. They loved teaching, and the love of teaching requires the love of learning, so all of them were great learners. However, the more you learn, the more you know. If you know more, it changes you in a good way; however, if you change, but the environment around you does not, that becomes an issue, one that, if not dealt with, means that the wisdom you have will result in destruction, and that was what happened to Rhondo D. Dron, Phloxia's dad.

Her dad, Rhondo D. Dron, was not always like what he became in his last years. He was very intelligent and worked as a teacher and wanted to always know more and do more. He would wake up earlier than everyone else, and while everyone was still in a deep sleep, he would read and read. Then he would write poems or plan for his life ahead, which involved doing something extraordinary that matched his intelligence.

Now, people in the land of Aliesalba believed in easy happiness, and easy happiness comes in one way, and that is to happily accept who you are, as you are, and keep living that way without seeking anything else or allowing yourself to seek anything else. Most importantly, you need to have people around you that think the same way as you, and, lastly, you need to make sure your surroundings are in harmony with who you are. There is nothing wrong with that. At end of the day, only one thing matters, and that is true happiness. If you get true happiness by shutting down your higher intellect, then it is great.

Rhondo D. Dron, however, could not do that, and the more he tried, the more problematic it became. His parents realised he was struggling and thought that having a woman in his life might solve the issue, and they suggested he should get married, an idea he accepted politely, for he may have wanted a different environment and new things, but he also wanted to respect his parents. To his surprise, it did work, at least for a few years.

After a few years, he had three daughters. He had stopped working, for he did not feel the same enjoyment as he had felt before, and he could not understand why. Simply, the reason was that he had still not accepted himself as he was, but he did not know that, and it led to great frustration for him, but not for his wife.

His wife, Abelia, was living as an Aliesalba lived. She gained satisfaction from what she had and enjoyed what life had to offer. Her husband's behaviour caused her happiness to dwindle, and that created the fights.

We have all experienced fights, small or big, and they have

only one meaning: that you want something different to what you have at the moment. To put it in simple words, you have changed, and so you want 'change'. Now, what that change is, might not be very difficult to figure out, but that is the second step, and most of us do not understand the first step, which is to realise that all the frustration that we feel is because we have changed—and something has caused us to change.

However, the fights between Rhondo D. Dron and his wife, Abelia, got worse and worse every passing day, and to kill the changed person, Rhondo D. Dron started to drink alcohol and people started calling him a drunk, which did not matter to him, for drinking made him indifferent to his surroundings, and his problem felt solved, and that created a problem for Abelia, for her surroundings became less satisfactory.

All this mess turned the D. Dron family from a prestigious family to a laughing stock, and, thus, Mr Fate had chosen the perfect family for Phloxia, the one that would only want to have husbands for all the daughters so as to settle them. This was very possible and imminent, until one day, Rhondo D. Dron passed away while passed out due to having a high dose of alcohol in his system.

The death of Rhondo D. Dron was so unexpected that the family had no idea what to do from there, and now, Phloxia was around thirteen years old, give or take a year.

Phloxia was born with immense powers within her, thanks to all the gods wanting her to win.

As:

• Magical love filled her with the tendency to fall in love with dreams and believe in them.

• Ms Destiny granted her more than enough willpower to follow her dreams and have a blazing desire to succeed in love.

- Mr Fate had given her desire to have family.
- The Evil of Hate does not give powers and only takes powers once one starts to have dark thoughts, Phloxia was prone to it for the God Of Humanity had filled her with good thoughts, openness towards life and positivity, no matter the circumstances.

But these powers, rather than making her confident and smart, made her shy and quiet to the extent that she did not know how to react to a situation or in an environment that was even a little unfamiliar to her. She was intelligent, no doubt, and a great reader, but rather than saying much, she tended to look at things without knowing what to say or how to react, and her lack of reaction to her environment was to such an extent that at her father's funeral, when everyone was crying, even the people who were not meant to cry, she was just looking into the distance, and I can assure you that she was only thinking one thing and that was: *How come I do not feel like crying?*

Anyhow, the turmoil passed, and Abelia realised that it would be difficult to find a partner for Phloxia for a very obvious reason: Her ignorance of her surroundings. Abelia may not have been as intelligent as Rhondo D. Dron; however, she knew that to live, one needs to have a basic understanding of the environment they are in and then adapt to that. There is no point expecting the environment to adapt to you, for it won't.

If Rhondo D. Dron knew the next part to it, he would be alive today, and that is that the environment won't change to meet your change; however, if your desire for change is strong enough, you are able to change your environment.

He might have theoretically known the first part, but Abelia knew it practically, and she knew that applying those principles was necessary for a happy life.

Anyhow, Abelia did not want her daughter Phloxia to be like Rhondo D. Dron, 'unhappy and confused'. So she decided to send Phloxia to get some valuable education. She wanted Phloxia to work and not find time to think unnecessarily or read and write useless stuff that only wastes time without bringing any food to the plate.

Abelia called Phloxia, and sat with her. She said, "My dear Phloxia, your sisters know how to react to the world around them and can have good husbands and happy lives; however, I am worried about you, and how to make you know the world around you, and, most importantly, to know what to say and do in everyday situations. I think it would be good for you to go out and get some education from the Institute of Theoretical Knowledge of Social Skills, make some friends, and learn to live and be happy with what you've got. Also, you might find a job as an educator later on, and that would help you find a desirable man, and you will not have to settle for an undesirable person."

Phloxia admired her mum's thoughts, for she knew that she did want something in life but did not know what. So, she reasoned, getting some education might enlighten her as to what she could seek and where to seek it, and if something was actually out there or if she was just experiencing confusing emotions inside her. She shared her thoughts with her mum.

Phloxia's thoughts did not make any sense to her mum and rather confused her, so she said. "As long as you can make a life for yourself and your family, that will be enough, and if you keep confusing yourself with what you just said to me, then you will end up like your dad. So think simple, be simple, and live simple, for nothing is more simple than simple." Then left Abelia to finish the daily chores, and Phloxia was left with her thoughts, which were simply blank, as Mr Fate wanted them to be, for Mr

Fate knew that no thoughts meant no ideas, and no ideas would lead her to just follow fate and not seek to change it.

Mr Fate worried a bit about Phloxia going to get some education; however, he did not pay much attention to that, for he thought that if her fate would not be to marry a man and have kids, then, ultimately, it would be the same as her dad's—death due to having education but not knowing what to do with it. So, either way, he was to win, and, thus, Mr Fate smiled at his own cleverness and how he was in control of others' lives.

"Equality,' he said. 'I am sure if Rhondo D. Dron was born in the land of Wellingtonia, he would succeed due to the help that is available to confused people." He laughed again at The God of Humanity for suggesting that he had given everyone equal opportunities.

Anyhow, Phloxia started to go to the Institute of Theoretical Knowledge of Social Skills, where she was expected to learn life lessons. Phloxia saw people around her and would look at them and observe them. So observation became the highlight of every day, for she observed her friends, and Mr Fate observed her. Mr Fate was very confused by her behaviour. *What is she doing?* he asked himself. *The gods have filled her with all sorts of powers so they can win, and she is standing there, just looking at everyone as if she is a below-average person. Clearly, something is wrong with her. I was thinking her fate would be to have a family, but by the looks of it, her fate is to be lost in the world and called mental and sent to a mental institution. But I decided she would have a family.* Mr Fate was puzzled. *Anyhow, if the mental institution becomes her destiny, still, I win. For Ms Destiny to win, she needs to spend her life with the other lovebird, who is in another world, tens of thousands of miles away, in the land of Wellingtonia, and there is no way a person of such a low IQ as* her would ever be able to make it to there, and if she does, then I might kill myself before I see that happen.

However, the odds were in favour of Mr Fate. He still decided to check out what was going on in Phloxia's mind. He assumed the appearance of a normal person and went to talk to Phloxia.

"Hi, Phloxia," he started. "I am Mr Fato." Mr Fate could not think of a better name in a hurry.

"Mr Fato?" repeated Phloxia. "I am simply Phloxia."

"I have been looking at you for a couple of days now, and you seem to not talk to anyone. Are you all right?"

"Yes, it seems I do not belong here, simply," said Phloxia.

"Do not belong here? But you are from here, aren't you?" asked Mr Fate.

"And that confuses me," said Phloxia. "Why don't I feel like I'm from here when I am here? Mr Fato, it confuses me too. Can I call you Fato?" asked Phloxia.

"Oh, yes, call me whatever," said Mr Fate. His heartbeat had quickened with fear, for if she was not feeling attached and attracted to the place she was currently in, she would start looking for other places to explore, and Mr Fate had to come up with something that would make her forget about that. He knew what he had to do next.

"Phloxia, do not worry. I will come up with a solution for you," said Mr Fato.

"But why are you worried about me, Fato?" asked Phloxia.

"I like to worry about others because others' worries do worry me a lot, especially yours. I feel very worried about your worries, especially your lack of thoughts about everyday life and how you only have thoughts about feelings."

Phloxia gave Fato a confused look.

"Oh, don't worry. As I was saying, I like to worry about others and especially you." And before it could become so awkward that Mr Fate would have to worry about the limited vocabulary he seemed to have today, he took leave from Phloxia with a promise to come back very soon.

Phloxia had doubts, but she let go of them, for she was confused about her own identity, and a confused person cannot make two and two, four, and Phloxia was so confused that she stuck at the 't' of the first 'two'. She was confused and was posing a danger to others, especially Mr Fate.

Mr Fate went straight to his next destination, which was to see The Evil of Hate, who was his only hope of gaining all the answers he sought.

The Evil of Hate was relaxed and observed life on earth from his chair high in the air. He saw Mr Fate rushing towards him out of nowhere. He had never known Mr Fate want to see him before, so he got up from his seat and walked towards Mr Fate, but before he could say anything, Mr Fate looked at him in surprise and said, "How could you rest here knowing that we are in a war-like situation, a battle of death and life? I do not know about you, but if I lose, that will be the end of my whole existence, the end of the whole meaning of my life, and the end of my world."

The Evil of Hate laughed and asked him to relax.

"How can I, when I see the lovebird Phloxia showing signs of estrangement? Before, I thought she was taciturn due to having a low IQ, but her feeling of estrangement is worrying me to an extent that I myself have started to feel lost and not in my world but, rather, find myself lost in her thoughts of estrangement."

"Relax, my dear friend, Mr Fate. There is nothing to worry about in terms of her behaviour. Perhaps you don't know anything about the scenario we have built for her, and I would like to have the pleasure of reminding you. She is the lovebird, and it is natural for her to seek her mate, and not any mate, but the other lovebird, who is in another world. She, however, does not know what she is seeking. You and I do, though, and if we do not take action in time, then the result will not be favourable to us, for the truth is, mixed feelings and strong emotions do end up making the impossible, possible. You are right, and we should treat the situation with the seriousness it deserves," said The Evil of Hate thoughtfully.

"I knew you would understand," said Mr Fate. "I knew it. For if I win, you win. I do not see any way she could end up in the land of Wellingtonia considering her destitute family and the fate I have designed for her. Still, she is a special case, so we need to be very cautious. I have never cared about anyone after deciding their fate, and only one in a thousand is able to change it to some extent. But who cares?" Mr Fate laughed.

"Let's get to work, then," said The Evil of Hate, for he understood that Fate was quite weak. A moment before, Fate was so panicked that his whole life seemed diminished to him, and after a minute of a talk, he was laughing. The Evil of Hate believed in winning, and only liked to hang around with people of the same calibre as him.

"I will give you the plan, and you will execute it. Do you agree, Mr Fate?" asked The Evil of Hate so as not to waste any of his precious time. "So, the plan is three simple words: 'Do your job'," said the Evil of Hate.

"Do my job? But that is what I have been doing, and she is

still showing signs that she will seek extraterritorial life."

'No, she is not seeking extraterritorial life. Rather, she is seeking an extra-terrestrial object, which you and I know does exist but she does not, and before she does, go and do your job. She has the fate of getting married and having kids, but before that happens, her sisters need to find their fates. How do you expect her to achieve what you want her to achieve without completing the groundwork? Isn't it the rule that the elder siblings find husbands first?" said The Evil of Hate.

It did make sense to Mr Fate. "I have been worried about Phloxia unnecessarily, whereas I need to make things good for the Drons in a way that enables the sisters to find husbands, for, by the looks of their current circumstances, it does not seem possible that they will do so without help from extraterritorial or extra-terrestrial forces—whichever one applies, as I do not have time to check the dictionary for my vocabulary. I will be their space inhabitant, though. Let's settle with this word- creature of space, creature floating through space to find husbands so as not to lose its inhabitant in time; that sounds better. The space inhabitant," said Mr Fate with a smile.

So Mr Fate decided to observe the D. Drons rather than Phloxia, for Phloxia seemed the least of his worries after his talk with The Evil of Hate.

D. Drons lived in a small village in Aliesalba; surrounded by lush green trees and farms of wheat. There were about twenty other houses in the village, and the mode of transport was mainly on foot or push bikes, and cars for longer distances. Public transport such as buses did exist but were rarely used, for people usually stayed in one place so why travel when the home has all the fun.

The Dron family were living their usual lives. Abelia was

busy doing everyday chores, which involved cooking, and the sisters were doing work around the home, which involved cleaning the clothes and washing the dishes. Then one of the sisters, whose name was Paulia, made tea for all of them, and as they sat to have it, there came the girls' uncle, Yarrow Dron.

Yarrow was of medium height and had a reputation in society, for he had chosen to stay single. Thus, he still had assets and money. He wore a white suit and had a styled beard and moustache.

Paulia brought another cup of tea and gave it to her uncle, for the family always made sure to make more tea than required. Even though they didn't have enough money, their hearts were spilling over with generosity.

"Where is Phloxia?" asked Yarrow, observing her absence.

"I decided she should go out and get some education, for she does not know how to behave around people. Even on the day of her dad's death, she did not cry, and everybody thought something might be wrong with her."

"So now that my brother is not in this world, you have started to make decisions about the Drons, Abelia?" asked Yarrow. "Remember, a girl out of the house on her own can only mean a compromised future, for no man will marry her if she has made friends with other males."

"I know, Yarrow, what you mean," said Abelia. "I want to have husbands for all my daughters, not only Phloxia. But now they do not have a father, and we are running short of money, so what kind of husbands are we thinking of? Paulia and Villiea still have the skills to make good lives possible, but Phloxia is not good at doing chores as simple as making tea; thus, having a little education might help her to get some work, and that would attract a desirable man to her."

"Hmm." Yarrow took a deep breath as if trying to understand the problem better. "Rhondo had the same problem as Phloxia. He was neither good at working at home nor outside the home; his talks were way too highbrow to make sense. The nonsense gene runs in the Dron family."

"I remember one of our grandads had a similar problem, and thank god, he chose to stay single and had no kids. Otherwise, we would be seeing multiple nonsense genes flourishing, and relatives talking about little green men that D Drons see, when others are asleep, and nobody else can see. So, it does make sense, and it is making me perturbed."

"However, now, I am the only wise man in the family, and I need to come up with something that will not make the Drons look bad. But before finding a solution for Phloxia, I will find husbands for Paulia and Villiea. Then I will see what is right for Phloxia, for, as their uncle, I do want a bright future for all of them. I better go now and talk to people around who have sons seeking wives." And with that said, Yarrow left in serious thought about finding two men, to start with, who were eligible for the role of husband. In fact, being single was the only requirement.

"This is my man," said Mr Fate, smiling and shaking his head in disbelief. "I was thinking about a way to do my job, and this man is ready to do it without being asked. These people might be short of money, but generosity is in their blood. Well, at least now I do not have to worry about anything. Yarrow Dron will find the husbands and seemed quite determined to correct Phloxia's course too. So I better have some rest from observing now, as it has been almost fifteen years since I have had proper rest, and once everything is settled here, I will go and see The Evil of Hate to give him the good news and tell him that I executed the plan even though Yarrow is doing my job without

being asked."

Then Mr Fate went to the Himalayas to seek peace for his eyes, which were strained after observing something for almost seventeen years without any practical involvement, and his eyes thanked him for his kind thought of going to the Himalayas.

For once, the D. Drons were not being watched by anyone, extraterritorial or extra-terrestrial, which was extraordinary in itself. And when Phloxia came back home, she was very happy, more than usual, more than expected, and more than she had ever been before.

"What is going on?" asked Paulia and Villiea. "We have always seen you at sea. How come your heart is at home today?"

"Oh my god, if I tell you that, you will both be astonished, for you would never have thought such a thing could happen, and not even in my wildest dreams did I think it was possible. I was being my usual self and staring at nothing, and out of nowhere, a lady approached me and asked what I was looking at. I simply told her that it seems as if I do not belong here, and guess what? She said that it happens, and it has happened before to people who are different, and there is another world— Wellingtonia, she said—and there are people there who are like me."

"The land of Wellingtonia? What are you talking about, Phloxia? You have started to sound like you used to."

"The land of Wellingtonia. The lady said that land has everything that we do not have here, and once I go there, I can come back any time, and we can get wealthy like we used to be. It is a land of dreams, the lady told me, and as she said that, I instantly felt as if it's the world I have been seeking; I knew there was more to life than having a family and kids. Believe me, Paulia. Believe me, Villiea." Phloxia was talking non-stop, as if she wanted to do all the talking that she had not done in her life till now.

Paulia and Villiea knew that their sister was a little on the mental side. She had the nonsense gene, as pointed out by their uncle, Yarrow Dron, earlier, so they thought it best to call their mum, Abelia, and let her handle the situation.

So they called Abelia home. She had gone to see the neighbours to catch up on the news of the day, for in their land, that was the only way to keep in touch with the world—through word of mouth.

When Abelia came back home, Paulia, who was good at telling stories, told Abelia of the nonsense Phloxia had been saying, but to her amazement, Abelia agreed that, yes, there was another world called Wellingtonia, for she kept up with the news every day and made sure to visit all the neighbours so as not to miss anything.

"I always wondered why I have been so interested in going around and getting news every day. It all makes sense today. It was for today, and for this reason. Your dad would always scold me for keeping up with the news, and most of the time, the issue was me not taking any days off from seeking the news; I wish he was here today to see the worth of my news-keeping hobby, for I just heard two weeks ago that a man from a village not so far from us went to another land about six months back, and when he came back, he had everything that we do not have, like a packet of coffee—coffee that is not tasty but healthy, he said. He also had something to cover his eyes so no one could tell who he was looking at, and a machine that answers his questions, and he called it 'ooggle'. But who was the lady?" asked Abelia, realising that, in the excitement of her great achievement, she had forgotten to follow the process of getting all the information and getting to the heart of the news.

"Her name was Ms Martini. She said that she was seeking people to go to the land of Wellingtonia. She herself was from there and has work that requires more people."

"What kind of work?" asked Abelia.

"Just simple work like cleaning the clothes, washing the dishes—things that we do at home every day," said Phloxia without showing any excitement about the work.

"But you do not know any of this. Thus, to me, your sisters seem better candidates," said Abelia, and Villiea and Paulia agreed.

"No, Mum, that is secondary. The main requirement is being someone who does not belong here and has a little education. Education is required, and that is the reason she came to our college." Phloxia felt proud saying that.

"Oh, Phloxia. I do not know if your uncle will say yes to it. Only today, he talked about taking charge of the situation and finding eligible husbands for your sisters."

"But, Mum, where was he when Dad needed help? No one is going to give us coffee, eye cover or ooggle. We have to get them ourselves, and life has presented the opportunity. You always worried that I would have a fate like Dad, so today is the day to change it. I have a feeling already that my life belongs in the land of Wellingtonia, and I should go, and if I do not like it, then I always can come back, like the man from the village that is not far from us, and if I like it, then I will still come back with all the things that he brought. Think how you would feel then. And rather than going around to get news, people would come to you to get news and give news."

"Mum, it is a promising future, and you always wanted that

for me, and that was the reason you sent me to get an education. It is your prayer that has been heard."

"Oh god, Phloxia. How much you are talking, as if you are making up for all the talking that you have never done in your life," said Villiea.

Paulia laughed, for she had thought the same thing earlier.

"What does getting to the land of dreams involve?" asked Abelia with a smile at the thought of Phloxia's bright luck.

Phloxia continued to try to convince her mother. "The process is quick and simple. It is going to take less than two months, Mum. The only requirement is that I pack and go," laughed Phloxia.

"It does not seem real," said Villiea, who had been quiet for a while. "How could that be possible?"

"It is just my luck," said Phloxia. "The ship is leaving in two months, and for some reason, one person pulled out, and that seat has been offered to me."

"Hmm, it seems like the D. Dron luck is back. We will be as wealthy and respected as we used to be before your dad's nonsense gene took over." That thought made Abelia sad, and she said, "What if your nonsense gene takes over you there? Who will look after you?"

"I will be leaving my nonsense gene with you, for it will not work in the land of Wellingtonia. It is a dream world, and only dreams come true there. Everything else becomes redundant."

"How will you convince Uncle Yarrow, Mum?" asked Paulia, afraid of losing all the happiness if their uncle was not convinced by the idea.

Abelia started thinking, and Villiea came up with a plan. "How about we do not say anything to Uncle Yarrow, for when he decides to do something or go somewhere, he does not tell us, so why do we have to tell him everything? Anyhow, he does not visit us that often, and, also, I am sure finding husbands for us was only an idea and will not offer any concrete results. It would be best to tell everyone after Phloxia is gone, or some people will not be happy."

All the ladies agreed with Villiea and prayed to God for happiness, success, and prosperity, before going to bed with thoughts of a bright future and good lives in their minds.

Phloxia could not sleep for thinking about how even the desire to go to the land of Wellingtonia had changed her in a good way. She was feeling happy, not sad, and found, not lost. *I am sure there is something there that is calling me and wanting me to be there. Maybe Dad belonged in the land of Wellingtonia too. Maybe all this stuff about having a nonsense gene is nonsense itself; I mean, who decides?* And then she remembered that her mum had told her about the answering machine called ooggle. *The first thing I am going to do in the land of Wellingtonia is get that answering machine and ask about the nonsense gene.* And lost in these thoughts, she found herself in Wellingtonia.

The land of Wellingtonia was beautiful and was filled with flowers of all imaginable colours. It had springs and birds that wanted to talk to you and did not fear you, and the people were kind and beautiful, so different from those in the land of Aliesalba. The first time she saw the ocean, with no end visible, there were two rainbows on each side that met in the middle. It was like God resided there. Then, from the ocean, a man came out, and that blinded her to everything else. He was so magnetic that Phloxia instantly felt attracted to him. She felt as if he was her opposite pole. That was the start of a dream, the beginning of her love story, the story she was reborn for, and the story the gods themselves were involved in. The dream that had seemed so impossible till now had started to show some prospects of coming true. This is what we all want—to create a dream we can aspire to—and Phloxia wished for that dream to come true. For the first time, she experienced feelings of love so strong that an urge to meet this magical man was aroused in her.

When she woke up in the morning, she chose to say nothing, for dreams are dreams and have nothing to do with reality. Even if not true, that was the belief she had, and dreams were a concept that her family linked to the nonsense gene.

The next day was a beautiful, shiny day with a slight drizzle now and then, even while it was sunny. They all started their morning routine of having tea and talking about the plans for the day.

"I will see Ms Martini again today and tell her that my family agreed to the suggestion, so she can formally sign me on. Once confirmed, we can start preparing for the big day," said Phloxia, finishing her tea and getting ready to go to the Institute of Theoretical Knowledge of Social Skills.

Her mum agreed and said she would also like to meet Ms Martini. She told Phloxia to ask her to visit them.

Phloxia said she would, and as she was about to leave, she looked at her dad's books and felt as if she wanted to read some, so she grabbed a random book and went.

Both Villiea and Paulia looked at each other and smiled as if silently remarking on how their sister had changed in a day.

Phloxia was very excited when she looked at the book and saw it was named *Hidden Love Language*. And as she had just experienced the feeling of love, she started reading the book on the way to the Institute of Theoretical Knowledge of Social Skills.

Love is a dream, a dream that we love the most. Love starts with a dream and continues after the dream comes true. Love never ends, and if it ends, it is not love. The dream that involves love is not the dream; it is life's way of matching us with our soulmates. There is a reason that we don't feel a magnetic force towards everyone. Have you ever felt so attracted to someone that even a magnet feels less magnetic to you? Have you ever felt that you have found meaning in your life, and from thereon, your only purpose is to have the magical magnet in your life? Have you ever felt that you do not need words to talk to the one you are attracted to, and that you both can understand what the other is saying without speaking? If the answer is yes, you have been using the 'love language' without knowing it. In this book, I will teach you more about the love language and how to attract your magnet by becoming a magnet. It must be a magnet with an opposite pole, or you will end up repelling your dream man or woman.

1.1 A love dream...

"Hmm." Phloxia was interested in reading more but realised she had arrived at the institute, and she had to tear herself away from the book.

Her only purpose in going there that day was to meet Ms Martini and convey to her that her family had agreed to send her to the land of Wellingtonia; however, Ms Martini was nowhere to be seen, and that gave Phloxia plenty of time to read more about the 'hidden language of love'.

Meanwhile, at her home, everyone was happy and admiring the luck of the D. Drons. "People have to struggle a lot to go to the land of Wellingtonia, and Phloxia has been offered a chance to go there out of nowhere," said Abelia. "God is listening to all my prayers of having a good life for all my children. Surely, the

Almighty will listen to my desire to find good-looking, well-settled husbands for both of you." Then she looked at Villiea and Paulia, who were doing everyday chores that involved cleaning dishes and washing clothes.

Paulia made tea, and they all started drinking tea and talking to each other about everyday life, and their uncle, Yarrow Dron, arrived. Paulia got tea for her uncle, for even they were short of money, their hearts always spilled over with generosity, like the tea was spilling from the cup, for Paulia, in her excitement, had filled it with more tea than it could hold.

Yarrow looked at the overflowing cup of tea and happiness that Paulia had brought, and everyone's glowing faces. "It seems the happy news got to you before I did," he said, taking a quick sip from the full cup of tea.

That took some of the happiness from the faces of the three ladies, for they were not expecting any news from Yarrow that would interfere with the plans they had for Phloxia.

"No, no, Yarrow, we have not heard anything. What is the news?" asked Abelia. She hid her excitement at Phloxia's plan to go to Wellingtonia under her wrinkles. These wrinkles were there due to her being in touch with the hot and cold of life. She didn't have bookish knowledge, but she had kept her heart and was fighting for her children even though Rhondo had decided to give up because of his fight with himself.

Yarrow then looked at the girls and said, "Get ready to move to a new house. I have found perfect, well-settled, and wealthy families for both of you. You are my daughters as much as your father was my brother. Even though the nonsense gene made his behaviour inexplicable towards his end, I loved him; he was knowledgeable. I am so glad my brother's daughters will go to such good families."

Abelia looked at both her daughters and smiled, for she was happy with the thought that Phloxia would go to the land of Wellingtonia, and her other daughters would get married. All the happiness had come at once.

"So, they ask for the wedding to be in the next two months," said Yarrow Dron. "Can it be arranged?"

"Do they need any dowry?" asked Abelia, for they were short of money.

"They do not, and even if they did, I am here to cover for my brother. His daughters are mine. Anyhow, I will come back with a fixed date, but it will be within two months, so start preparing," said Yarrow Dron and left.

As soon as Yarrow left, Abelia turned to her daughters and just smiled. As for her daughters, for now, they were not thinking about any of the difficulties that were to come in getting Phloxia to the land of Wellingtonia, for Ms Martini was helping her.

After hours of waiting, Ms Martini showed up to meet Phloxia, who was lost in *Hidden Love Language*. "You seem to have quite an interest in love," said Ms Martini.

"I started reading it, for my dad had this book in his library. I picked out a random book, and it turned out to be this one," said Phloxia as she pointed at the name of the book.

"When things happen to us out of nowhere that we wanted to happen, those are not called random things but magic," said Ms Martini with a smile.

Phloxia knew there was not any other book that would have been so meaningful to her, but she did not quite understand Ms Martini, and said that her family had agreed and wanted to know the exact process and plan to go to the land of Wellingtonia.

"It will take around two weeks, but I will try to make it as early as possible for you. You have to get some documents such as your birth certificate and the pass to the port, which will include all your information. When your pass to the port is ready, I can book you on the ship. Make sure it happens as quickly as possible, for if this ship leaves, we won't know when the next one is to come."

"Okay," said Phloxia. "I will make sure to have everything within days."

"I will come back and see you once you have everything," said Ms Martini.

"But how will I find you?" asked Phloxia.

"Like you found the book," said Ms Martini, smiling as her eyes shined, and then she left.

"*Magic*," said Phloxia and went back home.

At home, happy news was waiting. Her sisters' futures had been decided by fate and accepted by them.

Phloxia was happy to hear the news and asked if she would still be able to go to the land of her dreams.

"You can," said Abelia. "As long as we keep it quiet, and if you can't go, then you must remember that everything happens for a reason and take it as your destiny."

"I would not take it as my destiny. If anything, that would be my fate, and I am not letting fate overpower my destiny," said Phloxia, surprised to hear her own words. She asked herself where they were coming from, little knowing that all the powers within her had started to wake up after seeing the dream of the man she could meet. It all depended now on the war between the gods and their powers. However, still, it all had to be within her reach and in harmony with the universe. The dream could be a reality, even though a dream can become a reality but only if we accept the idea and are willing to put in all the effort needed to make that dream come true.

Phloxia had accepted the idea that she should go to Wellingtonia, but it would only be possible with the support of her family. At least, for now, it seemed possible and there was hope.

The game had started, and the twist was yet to come. The girls' uncle had gone to get the dates for the wedding, and Ms Martini was trying to fix the ship for Phloxia. Meanwhile, Mr Fate was away, trying to relieve his strained eyes.

As it all happened, Yarrow Dron came back and told Abelia that they would be ready in three weeks, and, yes, that was good news for Abelia and the D. Dron family, except Phloxia, who thought that if the dates clashed with her leaving, then it would be a disaster. However, that did not happen, and she was told by Ms Martini, after she handed her all the documents, that she could leave in two weeks.

"I will be gone before the wedding," said Phloxia.

And we can say it all happened so quickly that there was no time to tell anyone, thought, Abelia.

And, so, preparations began, mainly for the wedding, for Ms Martini was sorting out everything for Phloxia.

Now, it had been one month since Mr Fate left, give or take a week, and he decided to come back, for he had an inkling that something had been going on while he was away in the Himalayas. Also, his eyes were feeling much better and were now a little cold. Thus, Mr Fate realised that too much of anything was a problem, and had he not spent seventeen years watching Phloxia unnecessarily, he would not have needed to go to the Himalayas, and if he stayed there another month, then there might not be any point going back, for things would be so bad that he would not be able to fix them. That was his inkling.

He came back, and the first thing he did was visit the D. Drons, and when he did, he almost had a heart attack. *What on earth is going on?* There were preparations going on—new paint, new clothes, new dresses and so much more. *What are these preparations for? And how can the D. Drons afford them when they are short of money?* He had forgotten that their hearts were filled with generosity, and sometimes, that is all you need to buy goods. Regardless of whether that is true or not, thinking that way makes one feel good, and feeling good is all that matters.

Anyhow, Mr Fate changed himself to a gentleman by donning a suit, and he hid his eyes behind the things that let you look at everyone without being known by others. "I will get to the bottom of this," he said to himself and took off to see Abelia, who was at home when he got there. *Just my luck,* he thought, for Abelia was usually busy getting the news at that time of the day. Mr Fate knew her schedule by heart from keeping his eyes on the D. Drons for seventeen years.

"I am Mr Fato," he was about to say, but then he realised he had met Phloxia with that name before, and he did not want to do anything that would create any issues. "I am Mr Futho," he said instead.

"Okay," said Abelia, looking at him in surprise, for she was not expecting anyone, and by the look of it, he seemed to be from the land of Wellingtonia as he was wearing coloured eye covers, whose purpose was described earlier.

"I am here to help." As that was said by Mr Futho, Abelia thought he might be the one who had been helping Phloxia leave the land of Aliesalba, for she totally forgot about the name Phloxia had told her.

"Oh, come in," she said. "We are very pleased to see you, for you have been so generous to us. Everything is possible, and I had no idea that was so until you decided to help Phloxia. Does she need more help? I thought everything was set up; the documents are sent, and the date is set."

Mr Futho was confused. He gave Abelia a weird look, for who was she confusing him with? But before he could clarify anything, there came Yarrow, and as he looked at Mr Futho, he was suspicious, for he had heard that whenever there is a wedding, thieves try to confuse ladies to steal from them.

So Mr Yarrow was very direct when he asked, "Who are you, black-and-white man?" As he said this, he pointed at Mr Fate's black-and-white suit.

"I am Mr Futho," he said.

"I asked who you are, not your name," said Yarrow, getting angry.

Mr Futho did not know what to say. To Abelia, it was not a big deal for a stranger to be asking about the preparations, for that is what she did sometimes when getting news; however, Yarrow Dron was a man, and it was a big deal, in his opinion, for complete strangers to ask about your family, for he had never done that, and getting news was not his hobby and, rather, finding husbands was.

However, before Mr Futho could say anything, Abelia interjected, for she did not want Yarrow to know that Phloxia was leaving. "He is the man from the close-by village, and he has come from the land of Wellingtonia to tell us about it and to see if we are interested in sending Phloxia there, for they need people with the nonsense gene."

Abelia thought that, by saying this, she would also get to see how Yarrow reacted.

"The land of Wellingtonia?" said Yarrow Dron. "Hmm, I knew this was going to happen. Whenever thieves see rich people, they dress as Wellingtonians and come to steal by fraud. I have met the man from the close-by village, and he is not Futho. His name is Fato…"

"Really?" said Mr Futho. "I almost said that name; just my bad luck."

"Now, before your bad luck makes this the worst day of your life, go and never come back, and if I ever see you around this house again, then that will be the last day of your life, and that is not because that was to be your fate but because I will change the course of your life and make it your destiny," said Yarrow at once.

"The irony," Futho just said and left for his own good.

Yarrow then looked at Abelia and said, "Now, this house is a wedding house. There will be not one but two weddings, and these kinds of people will be coming here, for they live on fraud, so be careful, and I will try to stay around as much as I can."

Abelia nodded. She could not figure out what had happened and what to say. She was worried, though, for she did not know what to do next. Should she send Phloxia to the land of Wellingtonia or not? Should she tell Yarrow Dron about that or not? Should she let that kind of person in or not? The answers might seem straightforward, but Abelia was confused.

She waited for Phloxia and her other daughters to come back. They were out shopping to prepare for the big day. So when they came back, she started by saying, "A stranger came today."

"A stranger came today?" repeated Paulia.

"Yes, a strange man came today," said Abelia.

"A strange man came today?" repeated Villiea.

"Yes, a strange man with eye covers came today," said Abelia.

She looked at Phloxia, who said, "A strange man with eye covers? Does that mean a man from the land of Wellingtonia?"

Abelia was irritated by now, for the girls were not letting her finish what she was trying to say. So she said, "Someone from somewhere came today, and your uncle met him. I don't know who he was. I thought he must be someone to do with Phloxia; however, your uncle thinks he was a fraudster."

"So what?" asked Paulia.

"I am thinking of telling him that Phloxia is going to the land of Wellingtonia very soon."

"Phloxia is going to the land of Wellingtonia?" said Mr Fate, who had started to keep his eye on them again. "How and when did that happen? I have been away for only a month, give or take a week, and I am hearing that Phloxia is going to the land of Wellingtonia? So soon? So soon, we are going to lose? It might not be real." He slapped himself to make sure he was not dreaming, for he slept a lot in the Himalayas and had been dreaming about his win.

"It is real," he said and straightaway went to see The Evil of Hate.

Abelia and her family, oblivious to his presence, continued talking.

"Because if we do not tell him now and something bad happens, then who will I ask for help? I am a woman, and I will be to blame, so, Phloxia, I know you might not be happy, but I have to tell Yarrow Dron about this. He has been very caring to us recently. Also, how old are you? Just seventeen years. So who knows if the choice you are making is wrong?"

"But, Mum, you are over forty. You should know if it is wrong or right, shouldn't you?" questioned Phloxia.

"Phloxia, a week ago, you were confused like your dad, and the change you are showing is now worrying me. I mean, you are questioning my intelligence. I do not know who that woman is that you have been seeing, or what she has been doing to you."

"Some people want to take advantage of vulnerable young girls. It is my mistake that I started sending you to the life learning institution; from tomorrow, you will be staying at home, and whoever that person is, they will have to visit us if there is any chance for you to go. Also, unless that lady comes, take it as a no, and if she does, I have to tell your uncle about it and take his advice. He is your dad's brother…"

"But you never cared about Dad," said Phloxia.

"Enough! Before I totally reject your wish. Stop arguing and see if there is any prospect that the lady can visit us."

"Well, I don't know where to find her, but she did say that if I need her, I will find her like I found the book," said Phloxia, pointing at the book.

"*Hidden Language of Love*? Oh god, have you been reading this?" Abelia put her hand on her forehead in disbelief. "This is the book your dad was reading before he went completely psycho."

"Mum, that was *Hidden Wants and Dreams*," said Villiea.

"Oh dear God, forgive these ladies here or at least me; they have started reading things that are forbidden."

"Forbidden?" asked Paulia, who had never liked reading and was glad her mum was the same.

"Yes, dear Paulia, forbidden. Any book that has the word 'hidden' in it is not permitted, for only one thing is hidden, and that is evil; reading hidden stuff brings evil to life. I told your dad many times to get rid of these books, but he never cared and had to bear the consequences."

"You better get rid of it, Phloxia, and find something better to do in life. Help your sisters to do everyday chores such as cleaning clothes and washing dishes."

"Anyhow, I have a little headache now, Paulia. Oh, actually, Phloxia, go make some tea for all of us."

Phloxia looked unhappy, for she had never made tea before.

"Do it or I will never let you go to the land of whatever," said Abelia.

Phloxia realised there was still a prospect for her to go to the land of her dreams, so she started making tea.

What can I do now? she thought. *What if I end up staying here? But what is wrong with that?* she asked herself. *Both my sisters are here. But what about the magnetic man I saw in my dream?*

Dreams are lies, though. As it is said, 'Dreams are a way to take your happiness, for they make you want more and make you dissatisfied.' I had better leave it to fate now, for I don't even know where Ms Martini is, let alone who Ms Martini is.

Phloxia thought about how she had to her accept her reality, but that thought also scared her heart and soul, and she forgot that the tea was boiling. The tea came out of the pot, and then she realised what had happened.

"Her nonsense gene is seeking expression again," said Paulia, smiling and looking at her mum, Abelia, who had taken two headache pills so she could get some sleep and distract herself from people taking advantage of the family's vulnerability.

Phloxia, who somehow managed to get enough tea for everyone, saw Ms Martini walking to the door, and she could not have been happier. She smiled and asked her mum to get up from bed.

Her mum was half-asleep but still managed to come out and sit on the sofa to talk to Ms Martini, for there was no other option.

Paulia and Villiea also sat around the table, for they were already having tea.

They welcomed Ms Martini, and Phloxia's mum signalled for Phloxia to get tea for Ms Martini; however, Phloxia gave a hand signal to tell her that the extra tea had spilled out of the pot.

"When I make tea, there is always extra," said Paulia.

"No, no formalities," said Ms Martini and got ready to talk with the family.

Ms Martini said, "I am here to confirm a seat for Phloxia to the land of Wellingtonia." She looked at Abelia, who was looking drowsy, for she had taken a double dose of her sleeping pills.

"That's all right," said Abelia, for her brain was almost asleep, and she could not think of anything else to say. But then she thought for a minute, and a word that she had been thinking about a lot came to her mind, and she said, "But what about the vulnerability?"

"Vulnerability?" asked Ms Martini, looking confused and wanting more explanation.

"We, the D. Dron family, are vulnerable, for we are only women here and fear someone taking advantage of us. How can you assure us that won't happen?"

"Oh, no, no, you are taking me wrong," said Ms Martini. "I am here to help. I genuinely want to. Should I take it as a yes from you?"

All the daughters looked at Abelia for an answer, for that answer was to decide Phloxia's nonsense gene expression, for if she was to stay in the land of Aliesalba, it would express, and if she was to leave, then not, according to Paulia, who had earlier seen her spilling tea out of the pot after Abelia had put her decision to go to the land of Wellingtonia in jeopardy.

Abelia just wanted to go to bed and nodded in agreement. That made Ms Martini even happier than Phloxia.

"So we are leaving in two weeks. I will come and take you with me," said Ms Martini and left.

Abelia, without saying anything, went straight to bed, but before going to the bed, she took two more pills, for by now, her head was exploding with pain, which was caused by the pressure put on her by people who wanted good for either the D. Dron family or Phloxia, and she realised that decision-making was not a piece of cake.

On the other hand, Mr Fate got to The Evil of Hate, who was sitting on his chair in the air, and as he saw Mr Fate, he got up and moved to greet him.

"So, give me the good news, Mr Fate, that you executed the plan as I asked you to."

"I did not need to," said Mr Fate.

"Oh, how so?" asked The Evil of Hate.

"Their uncle, Yarrow Dron, was doing my job by finding husbands for the women."

"Oh, so, how did that go?" asked The Evil of Hate.

"I am sure the women are getting married," Mr Fate

answered.

"Then, that is a piece of good news according to your tongue, but your facial expressions are telling a different story. How so?"

"I heard Phloxia is going to the land of Wellingtonia in a couple of weeks, and I do not know how."

"Now, that is strange—not that she is leaving for the land of Wellingtonia, but that you don't know how." The Evil of Hate looked surprised and confused and lifted his right eyebrow high in the air like his chair.

"I knew you would be angry, my brother, The Evil of Hate, but I thought everything was under control, and it was when I left. Yarrow was doing my job, but when I came back, everything seemed so different. I mean, Yarrow did my job and found husbands for the two women, but Phloxia is going to the land of Wellingtonia, and I am confused," said Mr Fate.

"Well, Mr Fate, you are confusing me more than you are confusing yourself, and I am not your brother. In fact, I am not anyone's brother, and if I was, I would have killed my brother, and I might have already. Clarify what you mean by 'you left'. As far as I know, you have had your eyes on the D. Drons for seventeen long years so as not to miss anything. What happened there? Where did you go?"

"I had strained eyes, for they had been fixed on one family for fifteen long years, so I went to the Himalayas," said Mr Fate quietly. "And when I came back, I got the news about Phloxia's travel."

"Hmm, the Himalayas. A journey to the Himalayas gives peace to people but it took yours. Very strange. Anyhow, have you not tried to investigate yourself before approaching me to ask how that miracle happened?" asked The Evil of Hate without showing any signs of worry.

"I tried to but did not get any solid results, and I wanted to see you before it was too late, for I knew that you could do something about it, for your chair is in the air, and you are able to look around and see what is going on," said Mr Fate.

"Look, Mr Fate, understand one thing about me. I spread hate, and I am evil. I do keep an eye on things, but in Phloxia's scenario, I trusted your peepers, but that was my bad luck to trust strained eyes."

"Now, as I think with my evil brain, I realise there is only one explanation for this unexpected change. Ms Destiny must be involved. She would have realised that you were away and took her chance. That is the only way it can be explained."

"But rule number one was: 'Fair play and do not interfere physically; only watch till the end.' But maybe Ms Destiny used rule number three, which states that all of us are allowed to awaken her powers and make her utilise the powers that we have given her; whether she listens and uses them is up to her," said Mr Fate.

"Oh, well, Mr Fate, you seem to remember all the rules and can recite them in a parrot-like fashion. Though, it has to be rule number one that she has broken, for awakening is a piecemeal process. Here, what we are seeing seems supernatural, and someone supernatural must be involved, for extraterritorial life has become possible. There has to be one of us involved," said The Evil of Hate.

"Hmm, she was seeking extraterritorial life, as I had told you the last time, and maybe she has attracted it to her." Mr Fate looked suddenly very low-spirited and tired.

"I don't think, Mr Fate, you will be able to handle this all alone, so let's follow rule number four, which says we should talk to each other about any issues," suggested The Evil of Hate.

"No, we cannot do it just yet, for I have been physically involved, and unless it becomes critical, I would rather avoid it. I will try to find the answer and resolve it; if not, I will call in everyone. We have to soon anyway, as we agreed to meet after seventeen years."

"I trusted you the last time, Mr Fate. Do not mess it up, for as I told you, I would not even spare my brother. You are only a friend because we share the same goal for this mission: the thwarting of extraterritorial life and an extra-terrestrial object." The Evil of Hate laughed as he went back to his chair high in the air.

Mr Fate, taking no chances, took his peepers straight to the D. Dron house, where Abelia had just woken up after a long, deep sleep and asked Paulia to make tea.

Then she looked at Villiea, who was holding a book, as was Phloxia, and the only word visible to Abelia was 'hidden'. However, Abelia chose not to say anything, for she did not want to ruin her teatime, and also, as soon as both girls realised their mum was looking at them, they closed the books and sat around her to enjoy the teatime talk.

While drinking tea, Abelia said, 'We have two weddings in three weeks, so I want you all to be serious from now on and stop reading this unnecessary stuff that is only going to bring dissatisfaction to your life, if anything." However, as she talked, there came Yarrow Dron. Paulia saw her uncle coming and got up to get tea for him too, for Paulia always made sure to have more tea than needed.

"How is everything going?" asked Yarrow, looking at the girls and the books behind them.

But instead of the girls speaking, their mother answered.

"Everything is all right. I had a bit of a headache this morning, but now, after having some sleep and tea, it feels much better."

"I meant, how are the preparations for the wedding going?" asked Yarrow Dron again.

"Oh, very well, Yarrow. Everything is ready, and I am sure the girls are ready too." She looked at both Villiea and Paulia, and then she added, "Paulia certainly is, and Villiea, I am sure, will be soon, as I have already asked her to stop reading her dad's books."

"One cannot blame Villiea, for this gene of 'bibliophilism' runs in the D. Dron family as much as the nonsense gene. It is not as bad as the nonsense gene. However, the saint who tried to help my grandparents with the consequences of the nonsense gene told us that the nonsense gene expresses itself after the expression of the bibliophilic gene. So, yes, taking precautions is good—too late for Phloxia, but be careful about Villiea, for she is still sensible and has the wedding in three weeks."

"Yes, I do understand your concern, Yarrow. If I had known the D. Dron family had so many genes, then I would have chosen to get married to a different family. With God's grace, my family has no strange genes, and Paulia is just like me.'

Yarrow nodded to agree with Abelia and said, "Do not worry, though. I am also seeking a man for our dear Phloxia. I might have to find someone a little on the low-intellect side, but what can you do, when our dear Phloxia is unfortunate enough to have all the worrisome genes of the D. Drons?"

That reminded Abelia about Phloxia's journey to the land of Wellingtonia, and she said, "Yarrow, please do not mind." And she explained everything to him and told him Phloxia would be leaving in two weeks.

"That does not sound good to me," said Yarrow, looking worried. "Phloxia is only seventeen, and letting her go to a strange land without anyone with her does not seem like a sensible thing to do. Also, what would we tell the husbands-to-be of her sisters? Where will we say their sister-in-law went? And if we tell them the truth, I am not sure how will they react. I do not agree with this, Abelia," he said as he shook his head.

"I know, Yarrow. It does not sound too good to me either; however, since Phloxia has known about this, she has seemed to be acting normally, and I think it might be good for her, then, to go to another land. Also, that would lift the standards of the D. Dron family. She can always come back if she does not like it, and the lady said that she would go with her and make sure everything goes right for her."

"Hmm, I will leave that to you ladies, then," said Yarrow Dron. "If it makes Phloxia feel better, then it is not an issue for me, and I am sure her brothers-in-law will understand as long as they know that she will come back and will not find a man there to marry or, even worse, find a man without getting married. That is the only thing I want you to communicate to her, however possible. If writing it down on a piece of paper and making her read it as many times a day as possible works, then make sure to do it, but it has to get into her brain, which is blocked by two D. Dron signature genes."

"Thanks, Yarrow. I will make sure of it, and I like the idea of writing it on a piece of paper. Even better than her just reading it, would be making her write it thousands of times a day. That way, rather than reading books, she will be busy writing," said Abelia, looking both concerned and relieved with the solution.

'No, no, don't do that, Abelia,' said Yarrow in a high-pitched and nervous voice.

"Oh, did I say something wrong?" asked Abelia.

"The D. Drons have a third gene called the 'Pincel gene'. When it shows up, the Drons write and keep writing; that is the third stage of mentalism. You don't want Phloxia to get there, for none of the D. Drons have got there yet, and nobody knows the consequences."

"Oh, dear lord. The D. Dron genes are frightening me. I wish my parents had done a little research before finding Rhondo D. Dron for me."

"It is too late for that now, Abelia. Make sure to make her read our family values before it is too late," said Yarrow, looking at the picture of the very first Dron, who was famous for giving education to princes.

Mr Fate also shook his head in disbelief as he listened to the conversation and thought, *Yarrow, is my man if ever I need help; however, my first step is to find this lady who is organising the trip for Phloxia. I must make sure it never happens.*

Then Mr Fate left to find out more about Ms Martini.

Mr Fate now was on his way to find Ms Martini; however, there was only one easy way to find Ms Martini and that was to ask Yarrow, who he had declared was his man, and it was his good luck to see him standing next to a bottle shop. Mr Fate went to see Yarrow and asked him if he knew the whereabouts of Ms Martini, who had promised to take Phloxia to the land of Wellingtonia.

Yarrow had consumed a couple of drinks by then. He said, "I could not afford a martini." For even though he lived in the land of Aliesalba, he was still from the D. Dron family and knew how expensive such drinks were.

Mr Fate realised it was the wrong place and time to ask anything of Yarrow, but then an idea came to his mind, and it was the kind of mind-blowing idea that makes people use the phrase 'one-million-dollar idea'. *Why do I bother about anything? Why do I not delay the ship to start with, and wait for Ms Martini to show up?* He liked the idea.

So Mr Fate used his chums in the shipping industry and delayed the ship and, without wasting any time, went back to the D. Drons, for he had decided to watch them even if his eyes were strained. It was Mr Fate's fate that he saw Ms Martini sitting with the D. Drons and having their famous tea as soon as he got there. It did not take long for Mr Fate to realise that Ms Martini was actually Ms Destiny. Being an extra-terrestrial force himself, he knew that they had unique eyes that were bright, shiny and almost transparent.

Oh, no wonder. But she is unable to do anything now, for I have turned the tables in a way that, no matter what happens, poor Phloxia won't be able to go to the land of Wellingtonia. First, there will be a delay and then cancellation, which will disappoint her in a way that will make her so broken that she will not ever dare to think outside the D. Dron box again. By 'the box', he meant 'fate'.

Ms Martini looked at Phloxia and told her not to worry, for the ship had only been delayed for two weeks, and she would make sure that there would not be any delays after that.

Phloxia got a little sad, but her mum, Abelia, looked at Phloxia and said, "It is good, in a way, for you will be able to attend your sisters' weddings. There will be no questions from anywhere."

"I will come back after the wedding and personally take you to the port," said Ms Martini as she got up and left.

On the way, as she turned into Ms Destiny, Mr Fate stopped her and told her that it was not right to take advantage of her powers to become Ms Martini and show the D. Drons impossible dreams.

"Oh, so it was you who ruined my planning?" said Ms Destiny.

"Yes, ma'am, and I would like you to refrain from using your brain next time because I take my mission very seriously."

"But you have been on close watch of the D. Drons, so how could you blame me?" Ms Destiny was not taking her defeat easily.

"There is no use crying over spilt milk now, Ms Destiny. I am fate, the ultimate truth of this life. Don't you see everyone around you is living through me?"

"Rather, they are *surviving* you, to correct you, Mr Fate. This one girl—we want her to meet the man of her dreams, part of her own soul that we divided into two, her twin flame. Pity her, and let her win?"

"Not on my life," said Fate with a smile on his face.

"Hmm, then I am calling everyone in to meet. It is seventeen years anyway, so this is the time, for I need to know how to win, and I don't know how winning is possible without physically helping her, and until we all agree on something, we are not cancelling her ship."

"A gentleman would listen to a lady," said Fate.

"You are in no way a gentleman," returned Destiny.

"I hope you consider yourself a lady, though, that means you are more likely to be a loser."

"I can assure you that this one will be mine, by any means," said Destiny and left to get all the gods.

As the gods prepared to meet, the D. Dron family was getting ready for two upcoming weddings.

"Hmm, Phloxia, you have no luck at all. So many delays in your life," said Villiea.

Phloxia, who was overly sad about the news, said, "Well, you have all the luck, as others do, and it is making me jealous."

"Oh, dear Phloxia. Do not be jealous, for I will ask your uncle to find a husband for you too," said Abelia, who did not want the sisters to fight over a man.

"Pity me, Mum," said Phloxia. "Please do me a favour and don't involve anyone starting with 'y' in it."

"Phloxia, do not be such an unappreciative person, for your uncle is doing us a favour by making things easier for me."

"Easier? Does it matter? Things have to eventually happen anyway."

"Oh, then, Phloxia, tell me, why are you worried? If it is your fate to go to the land of Wellingtonia, then you will. You seem to want easy things too," said Paulia, who had been sitting quietly all the time and now wanted to take her mum's side.

"By the looks of it, my fate seems to be to end up like all of you. It is my destiny that is boiling my emotions," said Phloxia and went inside to read her book *Hidden Love Language*.

"She is reading again," said Villiea. "If you don't stop her, then I will read mine too."

"Yes, the whole family should go and get a book each and get the neighbours and give one to them too, for there is no shortage of books in this house, only a shortage of money."

"I liked Phloxia before she met Ms Martini; she would at least be quiet and do whatever we asked her to do," said Paulia.

"Except that she was on the verge of going insane, and there was talk about sending her to the mental institute rather than the life institute," Villiea said, smiling and winking at Paulia.

"Oh dear God, forgive them. Three women here making such a loud noise that your heaven must be shaking too."

"Four, Mum." Paulia could not stop herself from correcting her mum.

Her mum just asked Paulia to make tea while she was trying to read something peaceful from the Holy Book.

So Paulia followed her usual routine and made extra as a symbol of the family's generosity.

As the tea was boiling, Phloxia was reading the book.

When your emotions are boiling, only you can tell, for you will be feeling very hot, as your heart is on fire, and you have burning desires. In that magical moment, you feel precarious, for your soul is loose in the motion of the ocean, and if your feelings are not acted upon wisely or listened to properly, one can end up in the never-ending vicious circle, and all your life will be determined by the way others see you, for your vision will represent nothing but a short-sighted individual who is trying to and wants to look at the distance when nothing is out there. Everything is happening inside your sea, the sea of waves made of emotions and secret meanings.

Before Phloxia could read more, the tea was ready, and they all sat to drink it, and there came Uncle Yarrow. Paulia went to get tea for him too, for, in the house, there was never a shortage of tea.

Yarrow grabbed the tea and said that the wedding was to happen in the house tomorrow, and he would be sending men to do all the preparations, and he wanted the ladies to stay inside so as not to make anything go wrong.

"Oh, no, Yarrow, men are not the problem; the problem is the women here. They all fight so much with each other that it seems as if something will go wrong, and this wedding might not happen."

"Don't think like that, Abelia. I have got everything covered. The men who are coming here are all married and have kids, and if you want, I can ask their wives to come here too and help with the chores such as cooking and cleaning."

"That would be very kind, Yarrow Dron. That would be wise, for the only person I trust here is God and not even myself. I hope God makes sure that everything goes well."

"God will do that, and why would he not? The D. Drons have always followed all the rules, and if the faulty genes are in our family, that is not our fault."

"I admire your positivity, Yarrow. I will get everything ready for the wedding. My two daughters will leave me alone with Phloxia tomorrow. I am not sure I can handle that; it would have been good if she had left as planned. She does not even know how to make tea, and that scares me."

"Take it as an opportunity," said Yarrow, "to teach her the chores, for one day, she is going to have a family. You will not go with her. Or will you?"

"Well, Yarrow, rather than staying at home alone, I might go with her and make her family life easier by doing all the chores."

That made Yarrow angry, and he said, "I do not know about your family, but D. Dron women do not go with their daughters to teach chores."

Mr Fate, who had come back after inviting all the gods to meet, was listening to the conversation with his big ears and strained eyes. "Yarrow is my man," he said. "He will make sure that Phloxia gets married in time."

Ms Destiny was also watching the whole conversation unfolding, and said, "Abelia is my woman, for she always takes Phloxia's side, and if there comes a point where she needs some help, then Abelia is the answer."

"I am sure God will look after my Phloxia," said Abelia.

"Very closely," said Mr Fate.

"Right on your head," said Ms Destiny.

"God is listening, Abelia, for if he was not, then how would I find such good husbands? Darmar is very educated and has a huge business. His family is mostly out, for everyone works, so our Villiea is very lucky and will not have to do many chores, and by the looks of it, she does not like everyday chores as much as our Paulia does."

"Cornus, on the other hand, has a farm and a huge shop. That makes him a businessman too. Due to the farm, there is more cooking and cleaning involved than in Darmar's family, but our dear Paulia will deal with it, for I have seen her making tea, and it makes me happy. Every time I taste it, it reminds me of the head of our D. Dron family, the great-grandmother whose tea was famous in the town, and people would visit the D. Drons not to meet but to have tea. However, that became an issue in her later years, for she had not much strength left to make tea, but people would still come uninvited, so I would suggest that Paulia not make tea so tasty every day, only on every other day or when I am visiting." Yarrow Dron smiled and took a deep breath.

"Anyhow, I better go now, and I will come back tonight, for there will be a party and songs."

Abelia turned to her daughters and said, "Did you hear what your uncle had to say? Or do I need to repeat it?"

"We heard every word of it, Mum. Please don't repeat it," said the women and left, laughing, to go to their room.

"I can't believe I am getting married," said Paulia.

"Me neither," said Villiea.

"Hey, you, Phloxia, with the bibliophilism mutation," said Villiea. "Find a book on marriages and read us something interesting."

"There is a storybook here that has interesting wedding stories," said Phloxia.

"Read it, then. What are you waiting for? Christmas?" said Paulia.

"Hey, Villiea, close the door, for if mum hears anything, we will have to listen to a long lecture on the D. Dron values rather than the marriage story."

Villiea shut the door, and then Phloxia started.

"Once upon a time, a couple drove down a country road for several miles, not saying a word. An earlier discussion had led to an argument, and neither of them wanted to concede their position. As they passed a barnyard of mules and pigs, the husband asked sarcastically, 'Relatives of yours?'

'Yep,' the wife replied, 'in-laws.'"

The girls burst into laughter.

"Hey, life will be totally different from tomorrow for both of us," said Paulia, looking at Villiea.

"Yes, doing the same chores at a different place." And they laughed again.

"It is good in a way that we won't have to live with faulty genes, in case they are airborne." The girls laughed again.

"Stop roaring so loudly, or I am going to come and make you howl quietly," said their mum from outside to get the girls in order before the men and ladies came to help with the decorations.

"Just one last one," said Villiea.

"Wife: 'I look fat. Can you give me a compliment?'
Husband: 'You have perfect eyesight.'"

"I have one more for you, Paulia," said Villiea.

"The most important four words for a successful marriage: I'll do the dishes."

"At least you will be the happy one, Paulia," said Villiea.

"You will be happy too, if you stop reading about hidden desires," said Paulia.

The girls howled quietly so their mother did not hear, and they went to bed with hopes that they would start happy lives tomorrow.

The big day came, and the stage was set to have the girls married. Everyone was happy, except Yarrow, who was showing signs of worry, for managing the big day was his responsibility; however, he was closely supported by Mr Fate without his knowledge. The divine presence of extra-terrestrial forces created an environment of uncertainty around the D. Drons, for Abelia believed that happiness brings sadness with it, for no one can be happy to a significant extent without having a dark shadow around them.

So, as what you think tends to come true, there came the disastrous news. Yarrow walked to Abelia with a face showing a mixed expression of sadness and worry. "There is news…"

He had not yet finished his words, when Abelia said, with the same mixed expression of sadness and worry on her face, "I knew that was going to happen. I knew that something terrible was coming my way. I could just tell. I can feel a piece of bad news from a thousand miles away."

"Well, you certainly can, but it is not that far. They are just about fifty miles away rather than the thirty miles that they were supposed to be," Yarrow explained.

"What are you talking about, Yarrow? What is the bad news?"

"It is bad news. The grooms and their families are running a little late."

"Oh, that is not as bad as I thought," said Abelia.

"Hmm, not as bad as being a thousand miles away."

"That I said to explain my power of intuition," Abelia said.

"You do not understand, Abelia. In the same way that you get premonitions, I feel that something will happen—good or bad, I cannot tell, for I, too, am full of all kinds of emotions today, and a distinction is not possible."

"I know, Yarrow. I understand. What do you want me to do to make you feel better?"

"Ask Paulia to make tea, her signature tea. That is my only hope on this day of mixed emotions."

"I can arrange that to happen, Yarrow. Don't worry, and let me know if you want to know anything or need to tell me anything."

"I will do that, Abelia."

Abelia entered the girls' room and saw that Paulia and Villiea were ready with their new dresses, as was Phloxia.

Who should I ask to make tea? she thought. *If I ask Paulia, she might get her dress dirty, and the right person would be Phloxia, for even if anything goes wrong, it is not her day.* Hence, she looked at Phloxia and asked her to make a tea, and a good one, for Uncle Yarrow.

Phloxia said yes, for that was the only option available to

her.

Abelia, however, thought something terrible would happen, for she could smell lousy news from thousands of miles away. Still, she stood by her decision, as in her family, the tradition was to stand by one's decision, no matter how bad things got.

That is how I got married to Rhondo D. Dron, Abelia started thinking, for the wedding had brought memories back of her big day.

Her house had been decorated in the best possible way, with lights and fireworks arranged to happen after the wedding. Abelia recalled how she was standing in the big window, like the one in the fairy tales, and was waiting for her Prince Rhondo D. Dron to come. The air was filled with the scent of flowers specially brought from the town about five hundred miles away. They were brought at the request of Abelia, who could smell their scent, like bad news, from a distance.

Abelia could only smell happiness with her superpower until a crow started to caw near her window without any apparent reason and looked directly toward her house, and that put everything in limbo.

The caws of the crow struck her heart like lightning, and she felt electrocuted and fell out of the big window. That was it; that was the end of her happiness. Things were never the same again, for she knew the caws of a random crow had brought misfortune and blackened her future. She was not wrong, for it did happen, and she always had issues with Rhondo D. Dron or his family.

Anyhow, today, she had made sure to employ a special task force, some men wearing the same clothes as each other, to keep an eye out for crows and make sure that she would not have to hear a crow today. Still, Yarrow looked worried, and that was not making any sense to her.

If anything terrible happens, how bad could it be? Abelia thought. *The D. Drons have already lost Rhondo D. Dron. Phloxia is on the mental side. We are already short of money. The future is already uncertain, with not knowing if Phloxia will make tea or break the pot.* With that thought, Abelia went to check on her.

"So how is the future tracking?" she asked, for Abelia was still lost in her thoughts.

"What?" asked Phloxia, who was looking at the tea as if it was her lover from the land of Wellingtonia.

"What are you looking at?" asked Abelia.

"Tea, Mother. To make sure it does not boil."

Abelia looked at the tea and said, "It is ready; you better go and give it to your uncle, for it has been a while since he asked."

So Phloxia put the tea into a cup, and as usual, the cup was overflowing, and to her fortune or misfortune—we don't know yet, for there is long a way to go—there came the grooms with their families, right in front of her, and she saw a guy six feet, four inches tall, with a crow on his shoulder, walking towards her.

Phloxia was bewildered, for the guy with magical eyes in her dream had come out of the ocean in the land of Wellingtonia. However, this guy in front of her was coming out of the sea of people gathered to watch the big day unfold, and instead of magical eyes, a crow's eyes were looking at her.

And what everyone, especially Abelia, had feared, happened. The crow was so scared as it looked at the overflowing cup of tea, that it cawed. Phloxia dropped the cup and spilt all the tea on her dress. The crow guy came running towards Phloxia, caught her, and held her in his strong arms, for she was totally lost in the moment of disaster.

Phloxia gave him a strange look, but her mum gave him a distinctly threatening look, as if to ask, 'How dare you bring a crow into our house on the wedding day?'

But before Abelia could reveal her true feelings, Yarrow Dron came running and told her that he was Cyclamen, a distant brother to Paulia's almost-husband.

That did not cool down Abelia's anger, for this was not the first time she had heard a crow caw. She was lucky to be alive after falling out of the window of her four-storey house in her past near-death experience, which was due to a crow cawing, and she knew the worst had come. However, the best she could do was leave the room and cry in the sympathetic company of some ladies she knew from the news-collecting business.

Yarrow looked at Cyclamen, who was visibly shattered by the incident and had not intentionally done anything wrong.

"Don't worry, Cyclamen," said Yarrow Dron. "Her mum is very sensitive to crows."

"Oh, I thought she was angry because I touched Phloxia."

"No, that is all right. Abelia is all right with touch as long as it is brief and necessary."

Cyclamen looked at Phloxia and asked if he had hurt her.

Yarrow, instead, said, "She will be all right, and we should go and continue with the big day before anything else happens."

Phloxia, who had once experienced love in her dream, quickly got her book on hidden love language and opened it up to the page titled *'What is Real?'*

Real is what you feel, and not what you see. Real is what you believe, and not what you see. Something from your dream, which had you wondering for days without any apparent explanation or answers, shows up in front of you without any warning and seems unbelievable? It might be real or it might not be.

Real does not have any specific definition, so that complicates the situation. However, you don't know what is real, for when real love shows up, there is a universe talking to you, confirming its authenticity. So let yourself go and enjoy the ride until your true flame shows up.

Phloxia did not want to take it too seriously but still knew that something had happened to that guy, if not to her. *I am sure he has pierced his hand from a piece of the cup.* So she went to check on him, and she was right; he had cut his hand.

She cut a piece of her old dressing gown and made it look like a wound dressing, and they both smiled.

Yarrow looked at them, and his brain started to plan their union, one way or another; however, today was the day for Villiea and Paulia, so he told himself to concentrate on that.

The wedding ritual started, and the wedding ritual finished, and everything happened as it should, even though the crow had cawed, and that left Abelia wondering, for she knew that her beliefs had to come true, if not today, then tomorrow, and she shared her thoughts with Yarrow, who was visibly tired from the big day and just said that when it came, they would deal with it.

The two sisters departed the D. Dron house and left Abelia alone with just Phloxia to share her thoughts with.

Abelia was a very wise lady, with her own beliefs and values. One belief related to crows, but she had another one that explained a lot about her character and behaviour.

She believed that you should be satisfied with what you have and always look at the people with lower standards than you to make yourself feel good, for if you look up, then you will feel down.

To continue our story, after the wedding, she saw that Phloxia was feeling down and decided to share her values. "Look, Phloxia, the world we are living in is not very big, and, thus, we are too small to be noticed."

"What are you trying to say, Mother?" asked Phloxia, looking perplexed.

"Dear Phloxia, I realise that you are sad, for you want to become big, but because the D. Drons are short of money, that cannot be. However, I want you to be happy, so I am going to give you the golden rule to follow if you want to be content."

"What is that?" Now Phloxia was curious, even though she hardly agreed with anything her mother said.

"Phloxia, dear, always look down to feel up," Abelia said and paused.

"Mother, are you all right? And what is with the 'dear' thing, for you have never called me that before?"

"Oh, dear Phloxia, one of your aunts, who I usually don't look at, for she is up, attended the wedding and was using these words. I thought I should pick what I can from the people higher than me to lower them down."

"Oh god, Mother, you have gone completely mad today," said Phloxia, for she always had issues with her mother, but today, she was particularly exasperated, perhaps because now she had to bear all this alone.

"Phloxia, I have been trying to be nice, and now I am going to be straight with you. If you want to stay with me, I want you to be happy, and the only way is to look at people with lower standards than us. That will certainly make you happy."

"But, Mum, there is no one lower than us," said Phloxia.

"Then, from tomorrow, Phloxia, look around, and I assure you that you will find many, for I see them every day. Also, that hope of yours to go to the land of Wellingtonia will not come true. The crow that barked today gave me a hunch that it will not. So now I must tell you very clearly that this is my house, and if you live here, you must follow my rules."

"It is Dad's house," said Phloxia defensively.

"And I own it now that he has left for good."

Phloxia did not want to argue anymore, for she knew that in two more days, she would leave as Ms Martini had assured her.

"Whatever you say," said Phloxia and went to bed to get some sleep.

Abelia went to her room and thought that her talk had certainly convinced Phloxia to change her behaviour completely. Abelia was very proud of her pep talk on happiness.

Abelia, who had not attended school, which was not unusual for the ladies of the land of Aliesalba, was very confident and proud of her thoughts, values and beliefs, and today was the day she was appreciating her achievement of getting well-settled husbands for her daughters. Everyone at the wedding had praised her for that.

That had Abelia determined to change Phloxia to make her like Villiea and Paulia, particularly Paulia, which included becoming proficient at living at home, desiring a husband, then kids, and then accepting a big full stop with a permanent marker, for that is what the primitive instincts demand, and Phloxia would be made to follow their demands.

Another big day came when the gods met. The God of Humanity, Magical Love, Ms Destiny, Mr Fate, and The Evil of Hate were all there. They came from everywhere, and not only the gods, but also all of their chain of command, from the lowest to the highest rank, to see what was to happen, for the love story had become famous in both Hell and Heaven and was known as 'Twin Flame Love vs Gods'. Those on both sides wanted different things, and what they wanted was not based on whether they were from the realm of Heaven or Hell but varied according to what would benefit them individually.

Mr Fate looked at The God of Humanity and said, "It is not fair that Ms Destiny was physically involved to change the course of Phloxia's life, and also Ms Destiny won't let me do anything to stop her from going to the land of Wellingtonia. She broke the rules and must be punished."

"Did you not go to see her as Mr Fato?" questioned Ms Destiny.

And they both started fighting without saying anything anyone could understand.

"If things keep going the way they are going, I will never win," said Magical Love. "For even if she gets to Wellingtonia, there is no way she is going to even see the other lovebird, for he is a royal and is going to be the future king."

"Hmm, I am the winner unless any of you can come up with something," said The Evil of Hate and smiled, assuming an easy win.

Everyone looked at The God of Humanity as if to question his integrity, and now people from both sides of Heaven and Hell moved around in a circle and said, "If it is an official contest, then we are going to be part of it too, and the rules have to be very specific about who wins, as we are going to bet on the winner."

The God of Humanity looked at everyone and said, "We are playing with two innocent people's lives here, so we need to think carefully."

"You started this contest," said the other gods and everyone else. "You started it and will finish it with our consent."

"But we have to be fair in how we win," said Magical Love, who in no way saw himself winning in the battle of the D. Drons versus the royals or the land of Wellingtonia.

"I want a happy life for Phloxia," said The God of Humanity. "So, if her marriage is arranged and she has kids with that arranged man, then Mr Fate wins. If her marriage is a love marriage or she has kids with a man she loves and who loves her, then Magical Love wins. That is, to put it simply, when both parties are in love, and it is not a one-sided love. Are you both happy with that?" asked The God of Humanity.

"Yes, suits us," said both Mr Fate and Magical Love.

"What about me?" asked Ms Destiny.

"What do you want?" asked The God of Humanity.

Now Ms Destiny remembered the earlier words of Mr Fate. In essence, he had said that being a woman meant she was a loser, so she said, "I will not go for an easy win. I will play till the end and make sure Phloxia ends up with Deutzo Hydrang.'

"Oh, the other lovebird's name is Deutzo Hydrang? Thanks, Ms Destiny, for introducing our hero," said The Evil of Hate. "The great God of Pure Humanity has been very generous to offer an easy win to both Mr Fate and Magical Love, for they can win without exploring the land of Wellingtonia. I hope, though, he does not go easy on himself."

"I will not," said the great god. "I will, like Ms Destiny said, play till the end and will only win if Phloxia ends up with Deutzo Hydrang.

And that leaves me with one option. I win if you lose." He looked at both Magical Love and Mr Fate as if to say, "You are both on my side," said The Evil of Hate.

"So that settles it," said The Evil of Hate. "We meet when required from now on, although, from the looks of it, a win could come very soon if Magical Love takes things seriously, for, at the wedding, there was a guy who liked Phloxia."

"Oh, I remember. What about the ship that is leaving in two days?" asked Mr Fate.

"Anyone who is physically involved is still all right, but you cannot be holding her finger and walking her down the aisle. So, yes, you can see her, but as a human, and you cannot do anything supernatural to give her extra strength, and anyone doing that will be considered a loser and should accept their defeat or we will remove them from the competition and continue without them," said The God of Humanity.

So everyone was satisfied, and two gambling groups started with bets on each of the gods, and Mr Fate had good odds of winning. He bet on himself with all he had, without telling anyone or disclosing his identity. Now, it was not just the future of Phloxia and Deutzo Hydrang that was in question; it was also his future that was at stake.

So to feel better, he went to The Evil of Hate, for they had developed a great friendship thanks to the 'mission impossible'.

"Oh, I see the worry on your face," said The Evil of Hate, looking at Mr Fate and leaving his chair in the air, "when I thought there was nothing to worry about, for you will have an easy win."

"Easy win?" asked Mr Fate.

"Oh, so what is the difficulty?" asked the evil god.

"Her ship is in two days. How will I stop her from leaving?"

"Leave something to others too, Mr Fate. Are you not tired, for you have been managing everything on your own for seventeen long years?"

Mr Fate did not want to disclose his secret gambling to the evil god. "I trust you…" he began.

But before he could say anything more, the evil god said, "If you had trusted me, then you would not be here every other day with strained eyes and a sad face. Go and relax a little, for I am sure Magical Love has got it covered, for he would want to keep Phloxia at Aliesalba so to make her fall in love with Cyclamen, the crow man, remember?"

"Hmm," said Mr Fate.

And the evil god was right. Magical Love was on his way to find the man who had seen and liked Phloxia at her sisters' wedding with the hope of arousing feelings of love and desire to quicken the process of him falling madly for Phloxia, so madly that even a mad dog would feel inferior when chasing its desired mate on an abandoned farm to the barn.

This mad dog's name was Cyclamen, a name chosen for him by his mum because of her love for pushbikes and men. Nobody knew this, though, but for some reason, she told me when I insisted. He was interested in Phloxia, as we established earlier, and after Magical Love interfered in his unconsciousness using the magic potion, his psychological state changed completely, and now he wanted Phloxia at any cost, for the arousal was even more intense than Magical Love had thought. He only wanted Phloxia and no other woman.

That relieved Magical Love, for he had tried that on Yarrow in his youth with his newly discovered medicine, for Yarrow wanted to stay single, and Magical Love wanted to see if the potion he invented would change his mind. However, he was disappointed to see that Yarrow Dron never developed feelings of love. Rather, he ended up with a secret girlfriend, who left him after two days, and then he decided to stay single forever. So Magical Love made some changes to his original invention by making the potion three quarters love instead of the dose he'd had in his original formula.

Three-quarters of love did its work, and from then on, Magical Love called it a magic potion. And this is what he referred to it as when asked by Mr Fate, who trailed Magical Love's footsteps to make sure his future did not end in the darkness of the abandoned barn, whose door only opened when a mad dog went completely crazy.

"Do you think it will work?" asked Mr Fate.

"Do I think what will work?" questioned Magical Love.

"The magic potion?"

"It has already worked. Look at Cyclamen. His face is completely red, and he is walking around impatiently to find ways to get to Phloxia."

"There comes a man who will help to make it happen," said Magical Love, now nodding as if he had achieved what he wanted to.

"Who is the new arrival?" asked Mr Fate.

"Oh, you missed the wedding, for you were arranging for the gods to meet. He is Phloxia's brother-in-law, Cornus."

"Cornus?"

"Hmm, he loves bread made of corn flour." Magical Love

seemed irritated by Mr Fate's questions and asked him to write down any further ones he had, as Magical Love wanted to concentrate on his game. He was very affected by the success or failure of his magical potions, and even in Yarrow's case, when things did not go well, Magical Love had cried in the abandoned barn for two days and only came out when a mad dog showed up with its girlfriend.

This time, Magical Love did not want to cry, or did not want to cry in the abandoned barn, one or the other. It was paramount to stay focused.

Obviously, Cyclamen thought so too. He had told Cornus straightaway that he was in love with Phloxia and wanted to marry her as soon as possible. He asked Cornus how soon that could happen.

Cornus raised his eyebrows, for he had never seen or heard anything like that, and just said, "Are you out of your mind? These things take time."

"I don't have any," said Cyclamen. "I love her too much."

"I will convey your feelings to her when I go back home, for she is visiting me and her sister, Paulia, and if she likes you too, then I will talk to her mum, who, I am sure, will not have any major objection, for they all want Phloxia to have a family. That seems like an issue for them, as Paulia told me so on the first night, but by the looks of you, arranging it will be as easy as falling off a log in the abandoned barn."

"Oh, well, my mind switched off after I heard that Phloxia is at your place, and it does not matter what else you said, for I am coming with you to your house. Once Phloxia says yes, making her mum say yes will be like falling off a log in the abandoned barn," Cyclamen replied as he got ready to walk with him.

Cornus gave him a weird look, not because he claimed to not hear anything but was still repeating his words, but because he never asked him for tea, which was the symbol for welcoming guests.

Anyhow, they both looked very similar, for they were distant relatives, except that Cyclamen was six foot four, and Cornus was five foot four.

So Paulia saw two very unmatched individuals, not in thinking but only in size, careening towards their house. She called Phloxia to go and get the neighbours, for the ladies were alone at home, and Paulia could not tell if it was her husband, for it had only been a night since she had gotten married. Her in-laws weren't there, as they had already gone to say thank you to the man who had made it possible.

Phloxia rushed and got two ladies from the neighbourhood, and they looked at the approaching men and recognised them as non-dangerous individuals, for they were part of the Homosapien family.

"Yes, that is all right. Corno's full name is Corno D. Homo sapien." The two men were now very close. Their faces were visible, and they could be identified without the help of the ladies from the neighbourhood.

"Hmm, any issues?" asked Cornus D. Homo Sapien, looking at everyone's worried faces.

"Nothing, Cornus. To err is human, and Paulia has just joined the D. Homo Sapien family, so it is just a simple case of mistaken identity from a distance, a simple case of short-sightedness," said the daughter, who had just started reading *Hidden Words to Improve Your Visibility*.

Her mum gave her an angry look and took leave from the D. Homo Sapiens, for she had decided to go home and burn the book as one might burn the abandoned barn after it was of no use to anyone but mad dogs.

Anyhow, Cyclamen was very impatient, for he'd had the magic potion earlier and was desperate to tell Phloxia about the turmoil he was going through, oblivious to the fact that it was a game of the gods, and he was being used to save Mr Fate's future. However, Cornus stopped him from saying anything and pulled him closer, to Paulia's amazement, for on her first night, Cornus decided to play a maze puzzle with her. It was one he had been unable to solve all his life and was impressed to see that Paulia was a pro at it, so she got suspicious of the relationship between Cornus and Cyclamen.

Phloxia, however, was deep in thought as she was leaving in two days to somewhere that she had not seen, and she wanted to trust her feelings but was uneasy due to the number of faulty genes she had.

Paulia looked at Phloxia and said, "You seem lost in your thoughts like before you met Ms Martini."

"No, this time I know what my thoughts are," said Phloxia, coming back to reality.

They both then started doing chores, which involved washing clothes and cleaning dishes, and Paulia also put a pot on the gas to make tea, for tea is a symbol to welcome guests, while their eyes watched the super-secret talk between Cyclamen and Cornus from a distance.

Cornus stopped Cyclamen from approaching Phloxia directly by saying that it would be inappropriate, for women like Phloxia were so unpredictable that her own mother sent her to visit Paulia the day after the wedding because Phloxia was not following the lessons she was trying to teach her.

In her super-secret talk with Paulia, their mother asked her to teach Phloxia some lessons on family values.

"Phloxia has woken up and is walking with her head high and back straight, and there is no sign that she will back down from all this. All I can say is that she has decided to not follow my values. Paulia, I am sending her to you for a day before she leaves for another land. I do not want her to get into any trouble and bring shame to the D. Drons when on the land of whatever,"

Those were her mother's exact words, according to the women who had brought Phloxia to Paulia.

Cornus then looked at Cyclamen for a response.

"I still like her," said Cyclamen.

"What drug are you on?" asked Cornus, for he was surprised that a man could like a woman whose behaviour was so extreme that she would not even listen to her own mother. "That is pure evil," he said. "Only an evil woman could do that, for no other kind of woman would stoop so low."

"I do not know about the drug, Cornus, and, as you know, I only have a dad, and my mum left this world for good a couple of months ago, just as Phloxia's dad did. We are destined to meet. We have so much in common. We both only have one parent."

"You do not understand, Cyclamen, for marriage is a sensitive matter. If not handled with care, the information can leak outside to the world and cause a major disaster, like the Tipsy fruit juice disaster, remember how barrels of fruit and vegetable juices spilled into the streets caused by the collapse of a Tipsy's shed." Cornus was trying to convince Cyclamen.

"That was not too bad. That was all right; if there will be any such consequences, I am ready to bear them, for people got to drink free juice direct from the street."

"Well, if you are that driven, Cyclamen, I will leave it to you.

Go ahead and try your luck, and I wish you the best of luck."

And there went Cyclamen to try his luck, but he did not know that he would not need to put in much effort, for the stage was set by Magical Love and the situation was overlooked by Mr Fate.

"How do you think Cyclamen will stop Phloxia from leaving?" asked Mr Fate.

"Love is a bitch, my son," said Magical Love, looking at Mr Fate. "A man in love can and will do anything. I have seen people walking on fire for love."

"Oh, walking on fire," said Mr Fate, not looking surprised. "Taking a cold shower would be challenging, though."

Magical Love just shook his head in disbelief and turned his attention to the historical moment that was about to happen between Cyclamen and Phloxia.

"Phloxia, I love you," said Cyclamen abruptly and without emotion.

Phloxia looked at Cyclamen as she had looked at him on the wedding day, and he was the same—direct and to the point.

"Aha," said Phloxia, as if looking for some further explanation or information.

"That is all," said Cyclamen. "Please marry me."

"I don't know, Cyclamen. That kind of talk is forbidden in our family, like the books starting with the word 'hidden' are forbidden."

"But I heard you still read them," said Cyclamen, smiling.

"How would I know what you hear and what your sources are?" Phloxia did not like that Cyclamen had returned her words.

"The talk is not going as planned," said Mr Fate, looking at

Magical Love.

"Hmm," said Magical Love, rubbing his chin and little beard with his left hand.

"Oh, you are left-handed," said Mr Fate.

"Hmm," said Magical Love dismissively, for he was focused on the love talk, which was not showing any sign of love. But after a minute, he turned to Mr Fate and said, "We need a time-out, and to make Cyclamen more romantic."

"What can I do? We are forbidden to physically intervene, in our getup, I have to become Mr Fato or Mr Futho or something else."

"I am not talking about that, Shake things up a little. Go shake something. I have a plan."

Mr Fate shook the tree. Cornus suggested everyone should come and talk inside. And while everyone was distracted, Magical Love put a glass of water containing the magic potion right in front of Cyclamen.

Cyclamen was thirsty, and there was no denying that, but he did not want to leave Phloxia, and to everyone's astonishment, Phloxia felt thirsty too as she looked at the glass of water.

"I will get you another one," said Paulia as she realised that Phloxia was about to move to get the water.

"Oh, no, don't you worry," said Phloxia and drank the water. The magic potion went into Phloxia's digestive system, and then straight to her mind, and it changed her psychological state at once.

Mr Fate and Magical Love looked at each other and rolled their eyes, for there was no way to know how it would make her feel. Magical Love had never tried it on ladies before and the potion was designed to make a person fall in love with Phloxia as it had one portion of her name in it.

"Wait and watch," said Magical Love, rubbing his chin with his left hand.

"I am left-handed too," said Mr Fate.

"Great," said Magical Love and kept watching while rubbing his chin.

As soon as Phloxia drank the glass of water with the magical potion, her tone changed.

"Look, Cyclamen," she said. "You love me. I accept that. But you need to show me that you love me. Do something for me. These empty words do not fill my heart. My heart desires more, and you are acting like a fool."

Everyone looked at Phloxia in surprise, except Cyclamen. "I want to take you out to dinner tonight," he said.

"I am feeling strangely sleepy now, and my thinking is muddled, but I can go with you tomorrow. We can go out for breakfast." And straight after saying that, Phloxia went to bed.

Cyclamen looked at Cornus with a grin on his face.

Paulia could not make any sense of all that had happened and decided to cook dinner, for Phloxia would not be able to help now.

Phloxia, in her dream, went to the land of Wellingtonia and saw herself in a beautiful home next to a golf course with ocean views and surrounded by pine trees. There were two sofa beds in the yard with a table in the middle, and on the table were two glasses and a jug of water. Phloxia saw herself sitting on one side of the sofa, looking at the ocean and the pine trees. "It is a heaven," she said and wondered where her magnet was, and as she thought that, there he came from inside the house with two bottles of champagne in his hands.

Phloxia froze in the moment, and he spoke, "We are celebrating our first evening in our beautiful home. This is our dream come true."

Phloxia just kept looking and looking at him. Then she heard a voice. "He is waiting for you."

"But I am with my magnet," said Phloxia.

Before she could say or hear anything else, there was a splash of water on her.

"What?" Phloxia woke up from the dream, or the reality. Who knows? For it is said that dreams become realities when realities are dreams.

"I was supposed to teach you values and D. Dron beliefs, and you are not even following Homo Sapien culture. You are putting me in jeopardy. Mother has not sent you here to sleep, and now your invitation is waiting outside for breakfast. I'm not sure what I will tell Mother if asked. If I send you, then it will be an issue, and if I do not, then it is a problem. I am stressing about all this. The queen herself is sleeping without any worries. Learn something. At least learn that dreams are the biggest con of this life. The more you dream, the farther away you get from reality, and that creates all the problems. You sleep a lot, and that is the issue, for if you don't sleep, then you won't dream. I will tell Mum not to let you sleep."

"Hear what you are saying," interrupted Phloxia, for now, she wasn't even sure what she had been dreaming. All she knew was that reality was standing in front of her in the form of Paulia, and another reality was standing outside the door in the form of Cyclamen. Once she dealt with both, the most significant reality would be waiting for her at home in the form of her mother. In all of this, she did not know her own reality, and that was what no one was trying to understand, for she could not communicate it to anyone else. *How can I, when I have no idea if the question I ask is even supposed to be a question? The whole world is living with one reality, the reality of blending in with the environment they are in.*

So to face her current situation, she said, "Don't worry, Paulia. I will manage, or, better, I will marry Cyclamen, and that will make you all free from my worries and will allow me to blend in."

Paulia just turned her back, saying that she should thank Cyclamen for still being interested even after seeing and hearing a scene that could be a script for a drama movie.

Phloxia did not take long to get ready, for she knew that it was not about looking good. Rather, it was good to be looking for an option that could give her hope that she could have a life where she was free to do the things that she wanted to do.

Cyclamen was her hope.

Cyclamen took her to a nearby restaurant and ordered tea; however, Phloxia ordered a cup of coffee, for she wanted to change her taste.

"Phloxia, I know that you are challenging to deal with sometimes and can have thoughts that contradict the current reality, but I assure you that none of that would be an issue at my home because I only have a dad. When he gets drunk, he has the same trouble differentiating between what is real and what isn't. Also, he told me that when I get drunk, I have the same problem, so this story runs in our genes."

Phloxia just raised her eyebrows even though she was relieved to hear that Cyclamen was so tolerant.

"What is your family name?" asked Phloxia.

"D. Manhood, the best last name."

"Oh, that makes it easy to remember," said Phloxia.

"So, what do you say?" again asked Cyclamen.

"It does not even matter what I say, Cyclamen, for we are in the land of Aliesalba, and our parents will decide. In my case, my mum will make the final decision. It would have been better for you to take my mum out for breakfast. You are wasting your time by wandering around the wrong bush."

"Wandering around the wrong bush? But it is an important matter I am discussing with you." Cyclamen was feeling like he was not being taken seriously.

"I know, but that important matter is unimportant to me, for my mum is my god when it comes to living my life," Phloxia said.

"I don't know if I get it, or your basic knowledge is not at the standard of D. Manhood. However, she did mention that you have a tendency to act strangely when the faulty genes come into action. Thus, I can understand, for I am in love with you."

As he said that, Phloxia realised that Cyclamen was being serious, and she simply told him that she was leaving in a day to go to the land of Wellingtonia if her luck was not playing tennis somewhere, but she would be happy to spend her life with him if her mother agreed, and going to another land was not necessary, for how could she believe in something that she had not seen?

"I have a lot of options here and can, after marrying you, teach others how to excel in everyday chores."

Cyclamen was happy to hear that, and it seemed as if he could see his life unfolding with Phloxia. He promised that he would go and talk to her mum.

"I don't see any reason she would deny this proposal, for

marrying me would also stop you from going to a strange land. I am sure your mum wants this too."

Phloxia looked at Cyclamen properly for the first time, and thought to herself, *He does not seem like the one I see in my dreams. But, again, as it is said, believing in dreams is a way to live an unhappy life, forever. So I had better put a full stop after my dreams and start living in the reality that I have.*

When they got home, Cornus and Paulia were getting ready to go somewhere, and they asked Cyclamen about his plans.

"Oh, it's good you came back, Phloxia, for your mum called, and Villiea and her husband are coming to the D. Dron house today. You are leaving now so everyone wants to see you. Come. We are going there too."

Cyclamen looked at Cornus and told him that Phloxia had agreed that he could talk to her mum, so now the plan of her leaving for the land of Wellingtonia might change.

"We decided to get married, Cornus, and all I need is her mum's permission, which should come easily, so I am coming too."

Cornus talked to Paulia. Paulia did not seem to have any major objection, for Phloxia was an issue in the family and her marriage would be the solution. So they all took off to the D. Dron residence.

The end of one dream is the start of another. Dreams, do they ever end? Whether the things we dream of are small or big, don't we always have a gleam in our eyes for something that is out there, even though things 'out there' are not achieved without going 'in there' and exploring yourself from the inside? However, outside dreams or inside desires are yours to achieve. The problem is that it takes a lot to commit to one's dreams. So, for Phloxia, who had just turned seventeen, the dream of a magnet, a man who was trying to wake up her sleeping soul, seemed like nothing more than a delusion. It was time for a new dream, and her new dream was a life with Cyclamen D. Manhood.

Cyclamen is good too, she thought. *And I am sure he was in my dreams.* She kept looking at Cyclamen whenever she had the opportunity on the way to the D. Dron house and found that he was looking at her too.

He is good-looking, charming and well-off and, moreover, ready to compromise everything for me; what else do I want? He would make me happy and keep me happy, and I am sure of that. He loves me truly, and I am so fortunate to have him in my life.

On the way, they stopped for lunch, and Cyclamen made sure that Phloxia got the best seat and was served properly.

Yes, I am in love with Cyclamen, declared Phloxia to herself, and on rest of the way, she imagined her whole life with Cyclamen, while Magical Love and Mr Fate went to the Himalayas to celebrate their win, which they believed was imminent.

I will wake up late and ensure Cyclamen makes tea for me in the morning. Then I will do the cooking as much as I can, for he deserves at least well-cooked food. We will have a couple of kids, who will look at us as exemplary parents and will follow in our footsteps by having the same kind of lives when they are grown, and it will continue in coming generations until it becomes part of our genome, or it might already be. Phloxia was dreaming or thinking— whatever you think is right.

Cyclamen looked at Phloxia and imagined his life with her. *She will wake up early every morning and make tea for me, then cook for the whole family. We will have a couple of children, who will have bright futures like me. I will have a beautiful wife who serves me, and we will have no worries, as we will have everything, and there will be nothing else we want.*

Anyhow, with these thoughts, they got to the D. Dron residence, where there were a lot of people, including Villiea, her husband, Darmar, Yarrow Dron, and two other people that have not been introduced, yet do deserve an introduction.

To keep things simple, one is called A. Aunty, and the other one, U. Uncle. U. Uncle was Rhondo D. Dron's eldest brother, and A. Aunty was a sister-in-law.

A. Aunty and U. Uncle were the wealthiest D. Drons in terms of money, not heart. They visited Abelia only on rare occasions and had missed the wedding, for they were worried that Rhondo D. Dron's family was short of money and might ask for help, and they could not help, or to keep it simple, they *would* not, for they had a lot of wealth but were short of heart. It was not that Abelia had not invited them; she had, for Abelia believed that the presence of higher-status people made her look high, even though her eyes were on those who she considered to have lower status than her. Anyhow, in exchange for their attendance, they asked for the last piece of land Abelia owned. Abelia refused the offer, so they refused the wedding invitation. Today, however, they came because Phloxia was to go to the promising land, and they wanted to be part of the bright future and did not need any invitation for that.

Abelia was happy to see them, for she tended not to remember some things said by wealthy people, and, also, they were part of the D. Dron family, so there was no way she could refuse to see them.

There they were, everyone sitting on royal chairs, and everyone stood up to welcome Paulia and her party, except for Villiea, for she was making tea.

The waiting party seemed happy to see the arrived party, except for Abelia, who was surprised to see Cyclamen D. Manhood among them.

They all sat again on the royal chairs, which were especially borrowed for this extraordinary event. Yarrow started with the first sentence. "Phloxia, our child, you are leaving tomorrow, and we all are very happy that you will be accomplishing something that none of the D. Drons, to this day, has accomplished."

"We recognise the efforts of Abelia, for she supported you, even though that meant taking one of the greatest risks in the family's history. So, on this historic occasion, accept our congratulations. We also have here your A. Aunty and U. Uncle, who would like to give you a short and sweet lesson on the D. Dron values and ethics."

Phloxia knew that she had decided to cancel the plan and saw her life with Cyclamen now. Thus, she looked at Cyclamen and prepared to say something. However, before she could open her mouth to spill any words that would amaze the waiting party, A. Aunty stood up, moved towards Phloxia, hugged her, and started her lesson. "The D. Drons are not only humans, but they are living embodiments of traits that are almost extinct in today's society, including, but not limited to, love for family, love of kids, and love for spouses. I can clearly see that you are going to continue to hold on to the described principles even though you have been suffering from the faulty genes that D. Drons are unfortunate to have in their genome."

"God bless you, my child," said U. Uncle, and then there was silence for two minutes to acknowledge the highly regarded effort of A. Aunty. She sat proudly, with her dark maroon lipstick and face powder getting a little watery from the sweat on her face. The weather was hot, and, secondly, the tea vapour from the teacup was mixing with the hot air and causing droplets to settle on anything colder than they were. A. Aunty was a very cold individual when it came to feelings, and even though she had said warm words, that did not change her inside temperature, for she was indifferent towards Phloxia.

Now, Phloxia gave Cyclamen a serious look to encourage him to show the manhood he had displayed to her earlier when it was not even necessary. Now that there was a necessity, he was hiding it under his hood.

Cyclamen then collected all his courage and said five clear and simple words. "I want to marry Phloxia." However, no one in the D. Dron family understood these five clear and simple words and they had to be interpreted by Cornus D. Homo Sapien.

"Something happened when Phloxia was at our house, something that changed Phloxia's heart, and now she wants what all of us have; that is, a family and kids."

"What happened?" asked Yarrow, who was the first one to understand the change of heart, for it had happened to him when he had decided not to marry. He had wished for marriage his whole life, only to realise that marriage is a want that is pleasing from a distance, and the closer it comes, the clearer it is that it brings horror into one's peaceful life. It was the enlightenment he had gained after drinking the love potion, a trial of Magical Love.

Anyhow, Cornus simply answered, "Love happened. Love happened to Cyclamen and Phloxia, and they dream of a happy family, and permission from all of you is a way for them to turn their dreams into reality.'"

"What about going to the land of Wellingtonia?" asked Yarrow, for Yarrow was, no question, a man who still had an active brain, running like a horse. U. Uncle, on the other hand, was on pills to keep his mind and thoughts still after marriage, for D. Dron men have a tendency to do things that are inexplicable to their wives or anyone else who comes into direct contact with them.

"She does not want to go anymore," said Cyclamen D. Manhood, who was being direct in his conversation, in keeping with his name.

"I don't have any objection," said Yarrow Dron, looking at everyone. "It is rather good that she will stay here rather than wandering around doing things that are against D. Dron values."

A. Aunty and U. Uncle agreed with Yarrow, for staying here meant that Rhondo D. Dron's family would never be better than them, and ensuring that was one of their missions, out of many others.

"I need to talk to you, Yarrow," said Abelia to everyone's surprise, and Yarrow looked at Abelia in confusion. However, Abelia got up from her royal chair and moved towards the room that once belonged to Villiea and Paulia. Now its future depended on whether Phloxia left or stayed, for if Phloxia left, it would become a storage room, and if she stayed, it would be hers.

"I have an objection, Yarrow," said Abelia and continued talking. "I still remember that incident from the wedding when the caw of his pet crow reminded me of the most pleasing day turned horrible. He brought misfortunate to my daughters' weddings, and I will never forgive him. I would rather throw Phloxia in a well than have her marrying a man who keeps a crow on his shoulder."

"Am I hearing you right, Abelia, that you do not want this marriage to happen because of a crow?"

"It is not the crow that affects me so much; it is the roaring of the crow. That has already happened, and I know another disaster is to come." Abelia was serious.

"You need to let it go, Abelia. Cyclamen is a good man, and remember how we wanted a good wealthy man for her? And he is upfront about it. Sending her to the land of Wellingtonia is a risk of life and death proportions; here, she will live like all of us, and sleep like all of us, without any visions of something unreal that people tend to call dreams but we D. Drons call delusion."

"I know, Cyclamen, but it cannot happen." Abelia had a very prominent trait of stubbornness.

Once she had decided something, she would not change her decision.

Yarrow, who wanted the best for the D. Drons, called in Cyclamen to tell him to get rid of his crow.

Cyclamen looked at the unfolding situation, which was not making any sense to him. He had thought winning Phloxia would be an easy gig, but it was seeming tougher than the winning of Draupadi by Arjun in her Swayamvar, and he wanted to see if he had to hit the eye of the fish by looking for its shadow in the water.

But I never learned to use the bow and arrow, he was thinking. However, the task turned out to be the one that would change the way he looked at life forever.

"I want to be straight with you, Cyclamen," started Yarrow Dron. "Abelia does not like that you have a crow."

"But he is my godfather," answered Cyclamen, almost crying.

'Godfather?' Now that information left Yarrow questioning Cyclamen's mental state.

So, Cyclamen thought it was better to explain the whole thing. "So, it is like girls have fairy godmothers in stories or their dreams; I could not find any fairies anywhere, and also being a man, I chose a crow, which is a creature that is the opposite of fairies."

"He is the perfect candidate for Phloxia," said Yarrow, looking at Abelia and nodding.

"I still do not think that Phloxia can be happy with him. The cawing of the crow was similar to what I heard on my wedding day."

"Cawing of my crow? He only makes a gentle purr, if anything." replied Cyclamen

"Abelia and Cyclamen, fighting will not bring a solution, so we need to work something out. Listen, Abelia, you wanted to find a husband for Phloxia. Now Cyclamen is ready, and if you are worried about the crow, then he will never bring it to your house."

"I can do that," said Cyclamen. "And I had an inkling the other day that my future mother-in-law did not like it, so I have not brought it with me today either."

"So, what do you say, Abelia?" asked Yarrow.

"There is only one way it can happen; I want Phloxia to go tomorrow, and I will marry her to Cyclamen when she comes back. That way, I will not blame the crow for her misfortune, for she will have done what was planned before she met the crow."

"Are you okay to wait, Cyclamen?" asked Yarrow Dron.

And Cyclamen replied that he was, for he was on a love potion anyway.

They all then went outside and told everyone of the decision that had been made.

Phloxia did not look so happy, for when she dreamt of a normal life, her family wanted her to leave and try something different, and when she wanted to try something new, they wanted her to live with the already tested ways.

Anyhow, she did not have a choice. She had to accept the

decision, and she thought that it would give her a new perspective on life, and if everything went all right, then Cyclamen could join her in the new land. *A new life in a new land with the man of my dreams—what else could one want?* thought Phloxia, as if all her wishes had come true without even asking.

So that was settled, and both parties took their leave. A. Aunty and U. Uncle told Phloxia not to forget about them.

Cyclamen looked at Phloxia and promised her that he would wait for her, and the first thing they would do when she came back would be to get married. "It would have been done tomorrow if your mother did not have an allergy to my godfather," said Cyclamen D. Manhood.

"That's all right. The allergy will go away after I come back," said Phloxia, and they both smiled.

So, according to the new decision, Phloxia was leaving the next day for the unseen world. She had mixed feelings of happiness and nervousness and uncertainty about the new world.

The big, million-dollar question she was asking herself was, *What if I meet the man of my dreams there; will I be able to come back and marry Cyclamen?* But that question did not stay in her mind for long; she'd had a long day with many twists and turns, and she went straight to sleep, and to her amazement, she did not have any dreams that showed her upcoming life.

Rather, she had a scary dream, where she saw herself in a storm that was coming from two different directions, and she was on a boat.

The storm made her go in circles, and she was lost in the land of nowhere instead of being in the land of her dreams. That scared her to her soul, and she got up feeling frantic.

What was that about? she asked herself. *Am I going to die* on the way to the land of Wellingtonia? Or is it a sign that I should simply not go? But how can I, on the basis of my dreams, ask my mother to change her decision or change my decision? And in these thoughts, she slept and didn't wake again until the morning.

We will now fast-forward and skip the emotional scene that unfolded at the D. Dron house between Abelia and Phloxia because it was like both parties faked a bit of emotion with words like 'come back soon' and so on.

Anyhow, Phloxia got to the port and looked at the ocean for the first time. It was the most beautiful thing she had ever seen in her life.

Oh my god. I was about to say no to this heaven on the basis of my scary dream! If the ocean is so beautiful, imagine the world on the other side of it. I am so lucky to be able to do this.

And these thoughts again aroused her sleeping feelings for her magnet; however, as soon as they were aroused, she changed them and thought about Cyclamen. *Wait, what am I doing? I am going back in six months to marry Cyclamen, and here I am thinking about someone else, someone I haven't actually seen yet? What are these signs of? Cheating? Or insanity?*

Am I really crazy? How would I explain that to Cyclamen after six months? The poor thing will be waiting for me all these months with his eyes towards the land of Wellingtonia, and I will be cheating with someone else?

Wait, what is wrong with me? Thinking about someone who may or may not exist is not cheating; it is just a dream.

But how would I justify that dream to Cyclamen? Well, why do I have to? For unless you keep secrets, a marriage will end up in disaster. That was written in the Hidden Love Language book.

Well, there is another hour gone.

So she decided to read the book and see what it said about cheating and dreaming.

Dreaming is not cheating. However, cheating can be dreaming. At the end of the day, if cheating is what makes you happy, then what is wrong with that? However, it is wrong if you think it is wrong. The interesting point is, though, who is to decide right and wrong? It is you. You decide what is right or wrong, and if you are the kind of person who lets others make decisions for you, then it is even easier. Go and ask others, and if not, go and meditate for an hour. Then take a shower, have something to eat, and ask yourself this question. The first answer that comes to your still mind is the right answer for you, no matter how it affects others.

While Phloxia was busy reading the book, there was another situation unfolding. Magical Love and Mr Fate had come back from the Himalayas and found out that Phloxia was on her way to the forbidden land. That panicked both of them. They ran to the port and saw Phloxia reading the book and realised the ship was ready to leave very soon.

"How could this happen?" asked Magical Love. "I had a totally different plan."

"I know the answer," said Mr Fate.

"Explain it to me?"

"It is something to do with the Himalayas. The last time I went, my whole plan was turned upside down, and that was a seventeen-year plan. Yours was only a day-long," said Mr Fate in disbelief.

Magical Love did not understand much, for his facial expressions showed he was perplexed, and he asked Mr Fate to do something.

"Shake things up. We cannot let this happen. I mean, I will still be okay, although I might have to find someone in the distant land, but it is more dangerous for you."

"I will shake things up," said Mr Fate and shook a tree nearby.

"This is not going to work, "said Magical Love. "It is not Paulia's home that we want to shake. It is the ocean, don't you realise? We need shaking to a bigger extent. Shake the waters, strand the ships, break the buildings."

So Mr Fate did.

There were heavy storms from two sides. Phloxia was on the port, and she was so happy instead of being sad. *Dreams do come true,* she said to herself. *I saw it last night. Dreams come true.*

She could not stop saying that, and a lady walked next to her and said, "Only the scary ones." That took all the excitement away from Phloxia and fear took over.

The announcement came that the port would be closed for an indefinite period and passengers would be informed when it opened again.

What will I do now? She knew the only way left was to go back, but that did not sadden her too much, for Phloxia kind of wanted her trip to be cancelled so she could secure her future with Cyclamen, but she could not say that, for her mum was involved.

She had to wait for the storm to cease before heading back, and it was two days before she got back home. Her mum was surprised, and everyone gave their condolences. Even A. Aunty and U. Uncle sent their sympathies through a third party who regularly visited to give the news from the village to them, and from them to the village.

"So what is next for you?" asked her mother on the fifth day after she came back.

Well, Phloxia did not want to start the talk of her marriage, but her mother had left no option by not starting it first, so Phloxia hesitantly said, "I think it is all right now for me and Cyclamen to get married."

"Oh, you are still seeing that dream?" asked her mum.

"What do you mean, Mother?" asked Phloxia.

"You still don't believe me, Phloxia. When I said to never trust a man with a crow, I knew what I was talking about."

"But, Mother, you never said anything about trust, or have you changed your mind?"

"I have not, but Cyclamen has. He is already marrying someone else in a day," said her mother, looking indifferent.

"It cannot be true. You are just saying that because you do not want me to be with him. You are lying, Mum. I will not believe you until I see it with my own eyes." Phloxia almost cried.

"That I can arrange. An old lady from our village is going there to attend the wedding. Go with her and see for yourself. Your sister and brother-in-law will be there too, so it would not look odd either."

So she got ready to leave, and after the old lady came, both left to attend the wedding of Phloxia's husband-to-be in a chariot, and as soon as she got to the D. Manhood house, she realised that, yes, it was her husband-to-be getting married.

It shocked her to the extent that walking any further was like wading through quicksand.

She did see Cyclamen D. Manhood standing at some distance, and as she looked at him, he tried to avert his eyes and left the location.

Paulia, luckily, saw Phloxia and walked over to her. "Oh, dear Phloxia, we heard about what happened with the ship and hope you got our condolences."

"What is this?" asked Phloxia as if her brain had lost control of the language area.

"Oh, dear Phloxia, it is not your fault," said Paulia.

But before she could say anything else, Phloxia said, "I know it is not my fault."

"The Cyclamen do not have a mother, and they needed someone to do chores at home; his dad insisted that he could no longer make tea for the whole family all alone."

"But it has not been even a week yet, Paulia. I mean, Cyclamen was talking about love and spending our lives together. He said he was willing to wait as long as necessary, and now it has not even been seven days. How can I explain that to myself?" Phloxia was becoming frantic.

"You don't need to explain anything to anyone, Phloxia. Enjoy the wedding, dance a bit. The food is amazing, so forget about what happened. You will find someone better."

Paulia was right. That was the best Phloxia could do, for there was no way she could go back all by herself. She would have to wait for the old lady to be ready to leave, so she attended the wedding. Cyclamen never looked at her and it was obvious that he did not want to talk to her. That was the end of her first love story, just like that—or possibly her second if she counted the man in her dreams.

When she got back home that night with the old lady, her mother was waiting for her arrival.

"I was right, was I not?" asked her mother.

"Yes, you were, Mother."

"So now you believe that crows bring misfortune, don't you?"

"Yes, I do," said Phloxia reluctantly.

"Now you will agree to learn to do home chores, won't you?" asked her mother.

"Hmm," said Phloxia, trying not to answer but feeling like she had to say something.

"Now you know that looking down at people less fortunate than you is a way to stay happy and satisfied with life?"

"Okay," said Phloxia, although she was shaking her head in disagreement at the same time.

But her mother was determined to bring her point home, for it was a win for her ideology, and, also, Phloxia was not arguing with her, for she was a loser on all fronts today. But this next question from her mum was the real blow, for she asked, "So, from now on, you promise not to read any books with the word 'hidden' in them, don't you?"

Phloxia could not take anymore, and she did not say anything either. Rather, she went inside and got *The Hidden Language of Love* book and a couple of other random books, and she threw them in the yard, and set them on fire. She then went straight to her room that belonged to Villiea and Paulia before and locked it from the inside as her mum watched the book bonfire in the yard.

Abelia decided to not say anything more, for she knew that it was all right to cry over spilt milk, and off she went to get some news from the village.

Phloxia put her face in the pillow and cried and cried until there were no more tears. "Everyone wanted me not to go, so I gave loser Cyclamen a chance, and then everyone wanted me to go when I did not. But I still went and even questioned my integrity when I had a dream about some other man, and the ship was stranded, and that loser D. Manhood was cheating in reality without any remorse, and I AM THE ONE WHO IS CRYING; everyone else is happy. This is not fair. This is not fair in any way, God," said Phloxia and broke a couple of things.

By then, her mum had come back, and she told Phloxia to stop breaking things in the room, for they belonged to Villiea and Paulia.

"I am making tea," said Abelia. "If you want some, come out of the room."

By the time tea was ready, there came Yarrow, and Abelia got tea for him too, for she was like Paulia when it came to making more tea than required.

"What is going on with Phloxia?" asked Yarrow, hearing the cries and heavy breathing from the room.

"She is going mental because she realised that not listening to her mother will only bring defeat and nothing else. Truth is not as easy as a tea to consume," said Abelia, taking a sip of tea from her cup.

"What is the solution?" asked Yarrow, looking worried.
"I feel ashamed even saying this, but she needs a man. Find one for her as you found two before. I had thought she could stay with me for a few more years, but it does not seem like that can happen from the way she is behaving."

"I know, Abelia, but now everyone knows that she talked to Cyclamen amicably, so it might take a while before we find a husband. Make sure to keep her away from men's company now, for if she is seen with one more man, not a single man on earth will ever be ready to marry her."

"I know, Yarrow." And Abelia took a deep breath. "Rhondo D. Dron, your brother, was the same. He would go crazy when seeing any woman. She is more like him. I wish my family had investigated a bit, for the D. Drons are at fault in so many ways."

"You cannot blame Rhondo for this, Abelia, for I asked you to agree to marry Phloxia to Cyclamen straight-up, but you were too worried about his godfather crow. If it was not for you, Phloxia would be married by now. Anyhow, it is better to deal with it wisely. Try to be gentle with Phloxia. D. Drons respond to love more than anger." And with that said, Yarrow left and went on the lookout for one more husband for the D. Dron family.

In the morning, when Phloxia woke up, she decided to keep living life as it came, for when your dreams die, that's what you do, unless you die with them, for when night chooses not to turn into day, and day does not light you, and light only reminds you of the dark, then you know that you are dead.

Death is a vast subject. However, every day is a cruel reminder of unachievable dreams. Sometimes, living is more painful than death itself, so the only way one can live is by taking life as it comes and shutting the brain to any energy that tries to give fire to your dead dreams.

For Phloxia, however, it was the dream of marrying Cyclamen D. Manhood that was completely dead, but she was not very sad about it, for that dream was given life and light by extra-terrestrial forces. So she was sad about it, but no light could ignite it again, and no energy could awaken it.

She was, however, living with pain for the dream of a world that was unseen but seemed connected to her somehow. That was inexplicable to her but the dream was so real in her heart that when she destroyed it as she burned the book, it seemed she had also burned a part of her own existence.

What can you do, though? We are living in a world where seeing is believing, and believing in the unseen is a way to create dissatisfaction, even though it is not the unseen for the person themselves, for that person has seen it in dreams.

Anyhow, it is now a thing of the past for Phloxia, who decided to go with the flow, even though she did not know that going with the flow requires the kind of unquestioning commitment that only a person who truly believes in a conventional life can provide, and if you are forcing yourself to believe in this way of living, you are certainly going to question its ways, which is not allowed, for it has been tested over and over by millions of people who live that way successfully and never question a bit of it, and those who do, end up finding their own way. These successful few are examples to humanity and show that blending in might be good for survival but standing out is the way to live the life you want.

Phloxia, for now, was committed to the way of life her mother had asked her to accept. She woke up in the morning and made tea for her and her mother, much to the amazement of her mother, who was expecting her to be rather grumpy or sad.

"You seem all right today, son." This new way of addressing Phloxia was adopted by her mum after hearing it said by A. Aunty, who liked to sound different from other women, and her mum liked to learn new words from A. Aunty.

"Hmm," replied Phloxia.

"Don't worry, Phloxia. What happened is unfortunate, but I have talked to your uncle, and, soon, he will find a good-looking and well-off person for you, someone better than Cyclamen."

"Hmm," replied Phloxia.

Her mum got the impression Phloxia was not in the mood for answering her queries beyond 'hmm', so she changed her question by asking, "So what are you planning to do today? Going to the life institute is not an option anymore as it brought people such as Ms Martini into your life, and she brought nothing but distress to the D. Dron family."

Phloxia feared that if she stayed the whole day with her mum, then she might change her decision to lie low sooner rather than later. Thus, there was only one way to get away and make her decision solid as a rock so that no wind would be able to break it, and once that happened, she would come back, for then she would be a true non-thinker and would happily respond to all the questions and queries that seemed like nonsense to her now.

"I am thinking of visiting, Villiea, Mother, for I have not visited her yet," said Phloxia in a low tone.

Her mother thought for a minute, and then said, "Yes, you can go, but make sure you don't pull any nonsense there as you did at Paulia's, for it does not matter to you, but their in-laws took it as an act of extreme lack of good morals and character, which could affect your sisters' lives in their new environments, and they will be watched more closely by their in-laws than usual."

Phloxia wanted to go, and so instead of 'hmm', she extended her response by saying that she had learned that the men of the land of Aliesalba were not to be trusted, and that women should not be involved with them if they wanted to have peace in life. Thus, she would make sure to only enjoy the company of her sister for as long as she was there.

Abelia, thus, agreed to send her to Villiea and told her that her uncle would take her there that afternoon.

Phloxia's trip to go and see Villiea involved hearing Uncle

Yarrow Dron give her another lesson in D. Dron values, and it was nothing she hadn't heard before, for she was newly converted to the unthinking side of the D. Dron family. It took quite a lot of patience for her to not only stay calm but also smile. But she did it, for she wanted to get to her destination, which was Villiea's new home, and, finally, she arrived there.

It was a whole new world, as her brother-in-law's family name was D. Hidden Gem, and mentioning it was forbidden in the D. Dron house. That is the reason it took so long for Phloxia to say it. She could not stop reciting it, using her tongue in her mind, though, for it is said that forbidden things are the things you want to taste the most.

Phloxia felt as if she had come to a different planet. Phloxia had not seen the land of Wellingtonia, but she thought that if it turned out to be like this, then she would start to believe that everything happens for the best.

Villiea's in-laws had a bunch of buffaloes and a couple of cows, with some little ones standing next to them. The house was beautiful. There was no doubt about that. However, Villiea was covered in sweat in the kitchen making tea, and tried to look excited to see Phloxia.

"How are you feeling?" Phloxia asked Villiea.

"Feeling that my hidden wants and desires are to remain hidden forever or I will never be happy."

"What are you talking about, Villiea? It has only been a couple of days since you moved here."

"Hmm, maybe you are right. It takes time to adapt to new habitats. I am sure I will get used to it very soon, for we D. Drons believe in the survival of the fittest, and as it is said that life finds a way, so I will survive somehow by getting used to the circumstances and conditions that have been presented to me along with my new identity, Mrs Villiea Darmar D. Hidden Gem. The irony, Phloxia! I was interested in reading a forbidden book and got a husband with a forbidden word in his name. I warn you, Phloxia, to stop reading, or you will be like me, adapting to the new way of life Mother Nature has offered to you."

They both laughed.

"Oh, I already burned it last night. I had a little meltdown," said Phloxia.

"Oh dear, Phloxia. Are you feeling all right? For that was your dream, love and all. That was the reason you were learning the love language."

"Well, Villiea, don't we all dream about love? So what was special about it?"

"The special part, my dear little sister, Phloxia, was that you were believing in a man who only you had seen. You fell for a man who only existed in your dreams."

Phloxia took a deep breath, controlled her tears, and said, "Put some happy music on, and enjoy your new way of living."

"That is right, Phloxia, but my mother-in-law has an allergy to music, so I cannot do that. Music is forbidden in this house."

"Oh god, this forbidden thing is killing me," Phloxia said with a laugh.

"So what will you dream of from now on?" asked Villiea, looking at Phloxia, who was visibly trying to force herself to look happy by hiding her true emotions.

Villiea could understand her feelings, for Villiea was a dreamer too, and that was the reason she read books even though her mother had asked her not to. But she was more of a practical dreamer. Her philosophy was that if you dream of something, and it comes to you without using much force and energy or in an effortless way, then you should consider its viability and keep dreaming about it; however, if it is clear that the dream would require you to go against the flow, and that means you would have to expend a lot of force and energy, then the dream is obviously not viable, and the long-term results may possibly be negative, even after all the exertion. So, it is best to be wise and not give any air to fire and strangle your dream to death before you or others have to physically restrain you from walking on the path that leads to your dream. To be happy in the kind of society we are living in, you must become one of them. It means no one stops you from dreaming but will only permit you to live a dream that others can see too. Villiea was the wise one, a practical dreamer. So instead of thinking about love, she thought of marriage and falling in love with her husband, which was condoned by the civilization the D. Drons were living in.

So when she asked Phloxia what she would dream of from now on, she wanted to know if her sister had changed her dream to a more practical one, like she had.

Phloxia, instead of answering her question, asked her a question in return. "Have you fallen in love with your husband?"

Villiea smiled. "It takes time. For now, we have an excellent physical relationship, and that is all that matters."

"Is it all that matters, Villiea? I thought your dream was to fall in love with your husband?" asked Phloxia again.

"If you know that much about me, then I am sure that you also know that I change my dreams according to my truth. And for now, until I adapt, I wake up before four and sleep after eleven at night after doing whatever I am told to do all day long and acting delighted. The formula I am using is an actor's technique. Until I actually feel gleeful, I will stay upbeat without any music, for that is forbidden here due to the high level of toxicity that poses an increased health risk to the life of the lady that is sitting there looking at both of us talking and interpreting our words in her own way."

"Oh," said Phloxia, "you seem upset."

"Well, I am because my premonition has come true. You told that joke about how the four words needed for a happy marriage are 'I'll do the dishes', and I said these precise words to Paulia: 'At least you will be the happy one'. And there you go; she is. I wish I had said something about myself."

"Say them now, Villiea. Who knows? It could become your truth."

That did calm Villiea down a bit as she put tea in two cups and sat next to Phloxia to think about what to say, for she wanted to say something that would please her injured soul.

"I hope either their way of life changes or I change to their way of life," said Villiea.

That was not too much to ask, and who could blame Villiea? She was upset, and all she wanted was to be happy. So, what she asked for was not her dream but a way to be satisfied in her new life.

Anyhow, it did not seem that Phloxia was going to stay there for many days, but she had to stay for at least one day, for it was almost dark, and no one would allow her to travel before daybreak.

Phloxia engaged in light talk with Villiea about her husband, new clothes, jewellery and some old sisters' jokes, and that cheered Villiea.

Phloxia helped Villiea with cooking; thus, they managed to finish it about ten o'clock, and Villiea could sleep earlier than usual.

The following day, even though Villiea had woken up early, she was in a good mood or was merely following the actor's technique. Phloxia could not be sure, and she did not want to ask and upset her again.

Villiea, however, smiled and said, "Phloxia, I was distraught yesterday, but I am sure I will get used to it, for we D. Drons do not give up. I want to give you a piece of advice before you leave, and that is to dream and dream big, and go for what you want, but don't expect your dreams to become a reality." Then Villiea smiled again.

Phloxia got the message that you are all right as long as you think of dreams as only dreams, with no strings attached. Have dreams, whatever you want, but as soon as reality shows up, they are on their way, and you are on yours. You are nothing to fantasies, and dreams are nothing to you.

Phloxia did get a new perspective towards life, as she had wanted, and now she was on her way back home to apply newly learned skills and lessons.

Now, while Phloxia was on her way home, Mr Fate, Magical Love, and Ms Destiny were having lunch at The Evil of Hate's mansion in the air in a bid to end their rivalry and differences.

"I mean, what is the point of fighting with each other for nothing when she is doomed by fate already?" started The Evil of Hate.

"Hmm, we should mend our differences, for we are going to live forever, and Phloxia is going to die one day, anyway," Mr Fate said. "There is going to be one loser, and that is The God of Humanity, and the only delay will be in his acceptance that he has to give a speech of defeat."

They laughed again.

"You are not saying anything," observed The Evil of Hate, looking at Ms Destiny.

"I don't think it is fair that Phloxia has no chance to change her fate. She is surrounded by people who have the same thinking, and if she is doomed to live her fate, then why did The God of Humanity agree to bet on her?"

"Well, some things you realise after the bet. I sent him an invite for dinner, and he refused," The Evil of Hate said, taking more butter chicken.

"I had thought that love would win, but Cyclamen D. Manhood changed at the last minute."

"That was sad," said Ms Destiny, looking at Magical Love, who was enjoying the ice cream.

"Don't worry, Ms Destiny. I will not lose," said Magical Love, taking more ice cream. "For she is going to fall in love, one way or another. If not before marriage, then after marriage, with her husband, as her sisters decided."

"You are evil," said Ms Destiny.

"Hey, hey, Ms Destiny. If there is anyone evil here, then it is only me," said The Evil of Hate, laughing and eating butter chicken with the big spoons.

"Maybe Ms Destiny is angry, for she has no chance to win," Mr Fate commented, drinking red wine, and by now, he was onto his second bottle.

"I tell all of you, if there was no chance to win, then The God of Humanity would not take this chance, so don't be too happy."

Mr Fate moved one bottle of wine towards Ms Destiny and asked her to relax, saying, "Leave something to fate and sleep unconsciously with all your senses dead, for if you are conscious, you will only think of all of us."

Ms Destiny, instead, took the whisky bottle and put two big shots into her glass and drank. Then she looked at all of them and said, "You know what? Yes, you all deserve a celebration, but it is just the starting point. She has not even started walking yet, and you have already announced the winner."

Magical Love looked at Ms Destiny and smiled, enjoying the ice cream.

Ms Destiny offered him whisky, and he refused, saying he had never tried it before.

"Oh, you haven't?" Ms Destiny questioned.

"No, I am always high on love," said Magical Love, laughing.

"Oh, are you? Or you use the magic potion to get high, for your sole dose mixture does not seem to work these days."

"Well, Ms Destiny, for your information, I only use my sole dose when I have to force people to fall in love. If they are destined to be together, then there is no need for a love potion."

"What about if they are fated to be together?" asked Ms Destiny.

"No one is fated to be together, for fate means living a life in your comfort zone, and love resides outside comfort."

"Oh, that is interesting. Then how would you claim your win by forcing her to fall in love using a magic potion, you thief?" Ms Destiny was direct after having half a bottle of whisky.

"Ms Destiny, when I claim my prize, I will make sure to explain the authenticity of my win, especially to you." And Magical Love winked at Ms Destiny.

Mr Fate and The Evil of Hate were enjoying the food and music, saying, "At least no one is allergic to music here," for they had heard the conversation between Phloxia and Villiea earlier that day.

"Anyhow, time for bed," said The Evil of Hate, who had an exact bedtime.

Everyone else went home too, except Ms Destiny, who, instead, went to check on Phloxia, who had just gotten home and was drinking tea made by her mum.

"Satisfied?" asked her mum.

"Quite," said Phloxia and kept sitting there as Ms Destiny watched from her invisible cloak, sitting on a chair between them.

Abelia went quiet, for she knew that Phloxia would not answer, and then there came a random woman from the village. Abelia went to get tea for her, for Abelia also made sure to have extra tea.

"Did you hear, Abelia?" said the lady. "Someone saw two people of an unknown race, wearing masks, roaming the village at night."

"No, I did not hear that," said Abelia.

"Hmm, good, for I have not heard something like that for about twenty years now. We are safe."

"That is all that matters," said Abelia. "Did you actually hear anything, though?"

"I heard that the times are going to change. The night is going to become day, and day is going to become night."

"Where did you hear that from?" asked Abelia.

"My husband came home late last night and then started talking in his sleep," said the random woman.

"That is concerning," added Phloxia.

"Hmm, changing night and day's schedule is concerning,"

added Abelia.

"I meant her husband talking in his sleep was concerning," Phloxia said, laughing in a way that seemed a little hysterical.

The random woman got up, saying, "What I am going to say now is not what I have heard but what I have seen. Everyone says that Phloxia has faulty things in her, but I say that she is taken over by ghosts or dead souls. Look at her, Abelia. I better leave now, for seeing her scares me."

Abelia looked at Phloxia and did seem to feel a little scared too. "Go, son, have some rest. I might go out to dig deep into the hearsay."

"Wow," said Phloxia, laughing again.

"And make sure to keep your odd expressions to yourself when someone random is here, or I might have to take you to the ghost catcher, and that would be the start of a new era for the D.Drons, for you would be the first D. Dron to have a ghost in you. All the other D. Drons were in ghosts. D. Drons are famous for getting into ghosts and making them do things that they want them to do. Once your father made me cook his favourite meal by getting into a ghost."

"Mother, do you even know what you are saying?"

"That is what I am talking about. You lack attention and attentiveness. You don't listen to others. You are everything that a typical D. Dron is not."

"Okay, Mother. I will write an essay on a typical Dron in my own time. I am going to sleep for a while."

"Sleep and then eat, then sleep again, then wake up, then eat again; that is all you do."

"I just got back, Mother. What do you want me to do?" said Phloxia as Ms Destiny watched.

All this talk had made her sober and she asked herself, *What is going on? None of it makes sense at all.*

"I want you to stop thinking too much about what others say. Listen, and then give a response that is appropriate according to the situation. Don't start showing your teeth every time someone says something."

"That means, from now on, I will be doing what I am told to do?"

"That is what everyone does. That is the duty of offspring: to follow their parents. And in exchange, we keep you safe from dangers and provide you with the basic needs of life: food, a roof, and clothes."

"Mother, that is not going to work. You want me to play in your hands."

"I am the senior D. Dron here, so you must follow me. It is the rule. Also, you have nothing; everything here is mine, for I am the senior D. Dron."

"You are my mother," said Phloxia and laughed.

"Only for as long as you listen to me," replied Abelia.

"Why so much hate for your own daughter?" asked Ms Destiny, and to her surprise, Abelia replied.

"You never listen to anyone. Already you've had a crow-loving man in your life, and you are still laughing."

Phloxia thought it better to stay quiet, for it seemed her mum had high blood pressure issues.

That did work, and Abelia went to the village to hear more hearsay.

Phloxia looked at the bookshelf, and Ms Destiny looked at Phloxia. *Hmm, I don't think she can win like that, by just looking at the books, and if she loses, then I lose. I do need to shake things up a bit, give her a little blow, something to compare her life with.*

So Ms Destiny shook the tree outside.

"This is not going to work," said Magical Love, to her surprise. "I followed you to see what you are up to."

"I was only trying to help her," said Ms Destiny. "She is lost in the fight of us gods and does not know what to say or what not to say. I want her to find a book on Aliesalbian etiquette."

"Well, then shake the book cabinet instead; that might just work."

And so Ms Destiny did, but to her surprise, Phloxia did not care and went straight to sleep.

"She is all right," said Magical Love, escorting Ms Destiny to her home.

On the way to Ms Destiny's house, Magical Love kept thinking of ways to make things easier for Phloxia, but no idea was coming to her mind. He thought it would be good to talk to Ms Destiny and see if she could suggest something.

"Ms Destiny would it not be appropriate for us to do something in Wellingtonia to make life easy for Phloxia when and if she ever gets there," asked Magical love?

"What can we do there?" asked Ms Destiny.

"Well as you are aware of the situation in Wellingtonia, things have been dwindling for the people of Wellingtonia," mentioned Magical Love.

"Oh I have not been keeping track of Wellingtonia, what happened?" asked Ms Destiny. Thus, Magical Love took this opportunity to explain the situation to Ms Destiny.

The minor event that changed how things flourished in Wellingtonia was that King Father fell in love with another woman, and due to the high impact of his love, he left Queen

Mother and ran away with his lover to another corner of the earth. That mere incident was to change the whole course of Wellingtonia. Still, so far, it only changed the course of Queen Mother's life, for she decided to live in her room which others called a cocoon, due to Queen Mother not allowing anyone else in it. It was, though, a normal reaction due to the action of King Father and dealing with the feeling of desertedness. It lasted for days, weeks and then months, and Queen Mother stayed in her cocoon, which now the people around her started to infer as a shell, which they could not see past or through. Prince Deutzo, a handsome young man with a bright future, still had a bright future, but her emotions were dwindling. Queen Mother's sister and her husband mainly looked after the kingdom now, waiting for Queen Mother to come out of her voluntarily extended quarantine. So far, Wellingtonia still was as before rich, beautiful and flourishing, and primarily standard, and everyone had normal genes or, say, normal genome, a mix of recessive and dominant genes. No one had noticed any faulty genes like the one D Drons had; thus, Wellingtonia, a dreamland, was for people in Aliesalba.

"Oh that is big news," reacted Ms Destiny.

"It is and, so, as we know, Queen Mother is in her shell, Prince Deutzo Hydrang will only marry a princess, so far, I mean. I am sure there should be talks about his marriage already, so why don't we shake things to the extent that would allow Phloxia to have a chance by luck?" Magical Love suggested.

"Hmm, SHAKING THE ROYALS OF WELLINGTONIA? To successfully do the shaking, one might need to recruit one of the mad dogs from Wellingtonia," and laughed Ms Destiny.

"Oh wow, Ms Destiny, you made it easy. That is perfect; let's recruit a mad dog and shake Wellingtonia."

"Are you serious?" asked Ms Destiny, "And how would he

shake the royals of Wellingtonia?"

"Let's recruit him first and see what his calibre is," said Magical Love dropping Ms Destiny off at her home with a promise to talk to one of the mad dogs who were daring and could do anything if they decided something to be done.

Ms Destiny went to bed thinking what could a mad dog possibly do to shake Royals of Wellingtonia? However, that was not what she was worried about yet. Her main worry was to get Phloxia to Wellingtonia, so she instead decided to focus on that and have a good night's sleep, which is paramount for gods to have good focus during the day.

To keep his words, Magical Love went to see a mad dog and asked him for help.

"How could I help?", asked one of the senior mad dogs whose name was Mad Solo, who was sitting on the highest building in Aliesalba, in a little room filled with chemicals for he was researching the effect of the genome on behaviour. He was intrigued by how little differences in the genome were responsible for huge changes, like one to call a mad dog and the other to be a human.

"Please do what you can do. I have promised my love interest that you would do something." Magical love told him the truth. Thus, Mad Solo said that he would not promise, but he would do what he could do and he also mentioned that he lived in Wellingtonia once and so had friends there. So that was a good opportunity for him to catch up with his friends too.

That was assuring for Magical Love, and he got back to the current situation of Phloxia and her hidden love life.

However, now Mad Solo was thinking about how to help, for he was the man of his word, and thus, to keep his words, he decided to go to Wellingtonia and check out what was going on there and what needed shaking.

A mad dog to help Gods: that will be amusing! he thought and laughed, *what if it actually turns out to be humorous?*

Absorbed in those thoughts, he finally arrived at Wellingtonia. People were living happily. Men would go to work, and so would women. *What could I shake to make things easier for Phloxia?* He kept thinking. *Let's wander around for a couple of days, observe, infer and then decide.*

In the Palace, The Queen Mother was still in her shell. He decided to stay around and look at Wellingtonia for a couple of days. While he was visiting around, everyone noticed his presence and were alerted, for Mad Solo's arrival was like the quietness before a big storm. That made all the insects including spiders run for their safety from upcoming storms, not from Mad Solo in particular.

One of the black widow spiders who was knocking the stuffing out of male spiders after copulating, got distracted due to the news of impending evil. Seeing that as an opportunity, one of the male spiders on her death row thus managed to escape. But to his misfortune, he went straight out from one devils-den to another. He entered the hard shell occupied by the Queen Mother. As the escapee male spider did that, he saw Queen Mother, and without putting any thoughts into it, he went straight to his primitive instincts and bit her. However, he did not realise that Queen Mother had resided in that shell for months, and was filled with all kinds of emotions; anger, frustration, love-hate. And the result was that after he did his part by biting the Queen Mother, the Queen Mother did her part and knocked the daylight out of that spider at once. As soon as Queen Mother did that, it changed her whole DNA, and all the recessive genes turned into dominant genes. Queen Mother became the first woman to have an all-dominant genome. That little event that happened in the little shell changed the whole course of Wellingtonia.

The knockout was heard in the whole world. So as Mad Solo heard it and could not believe what he heard. Mad Solo decided to pay a visit to the Queen Mother to see the lady whose genome has been altered. Also, he was recruited by Magical Love to shake things in Wellingtonia, so how else he could shake things when the main tree was shaken to its core already, and meeting the main trunk was only his option to further intervene in the situation.

Mad Solo appeared in the shell, looked at the Queen Mother, who was still coming to terms with her new bold look and sharp thoughts. After looking at the Queen Mother, he realised that Queen Mother indeed had received all dominant genome. Thus, he said that 'my lord, you are bestowed with deadly powers, and you will be the only woman of a super calibre of all dominant genome'.

Mad Solo asked Queen Mother to pray for the dead spider and told her that in fact a male spider had escaped from the death row of a black widow spider, so give peace to his soul by praying and celebrating his powers in her.

On that day, after months, the Queen Mother came out of her shell with a hard shell on her body. She looked at all the men in her palace and announced them weak having recessive genomes. She used her powers to bestow the women of Wellingtonia with dominance, though Queen Mother was the only woman with all dominant genomes. However, the women of Wellingtonia now had most of the dominant genes, enough to follow the Queen Mother's instructions.

She sat on her royal chair and announced that from today onwards, all married men after mating must leave their homes and reside in wilds. Before leaving, their wives would pierce their ears and put one earring as a reminder of their marriage. The first one to go was the Queen Mother's sister's husband. The women of Wellingtonia were all right with the news, for the Queen Mother had bestowed them with part of her dominance.

Men were initially happy with their newly gained freedom, though, after a couple of months of living around an abandoned lake, they started thinking about the ways to get rid of the dominant genome. They did not have superpowers and thus could not approach the queen, but it turned out that the Queen's sister's husband was friends with Mad Solo who had been alone all his life doing weird experiments on genomes. He was an amateur scientist, and the Queen's sister's husband had also heard that he was back in the town.

So he said to all the men around the lake, "I have a friend, named Mad Solo. He is a highly regarded scientist in his own room. He will sure to look at the Queen Mother's situation and would find a solution that she could drink and get her normal genome back."

All men cheered and started waiting for Mad Solo's arrival, and, till then decided to keep enjoying their newly gained freedom from dominant women.

Prince Deutzo was still living in the palace full of women, for all men were sent out to the wild. He knew his time was to come too and felt emotionally very vulnerable. The Queen Mother now looked at him only as a man with weakness, even though he tried to explain what he could do if his genome was not as good as the women of Wellingtonia, who only got dominant genome because of her blessings.

However, Queen Mother was a woman now with dominant emotions and looked at everyone equally, and rules were the same. Prince Deutzo Hydrang must leave the palace after marriage.

Prince Deutzo did talk to the men in the wild, and they assured him that Mad Solo was on his way and would do something to get rid of the all dominant genome. Thus all men in Wellingtonia started to live in hope, around an abandoned empty lake doing everyday chores which were mainly washing clothes and cleaning dishes.

Some lived in caravans, and some had learnt to live in trees. Some learned to make fire, and some still have match sticks from home. No matter how things were, they were in high spirits, and would enjoy their life with whatever they had, like organising BBQs at night, live music and songs.

Wellingtonia's life course, where once happy royals lived, now had ruling women over men. When the Evil of Hate saw it, he summoned Mr. Fate to ask for his explanation, for this was not a twist but a full-on event by a spider who had changed the map of Wellingtonia. He had no idea if that would help Phloxia or not, but what happened was too hard to believe, and he wanted to make sense of it before starting to think of its consequences.

Mr. Fate arrived, and he knew what the question was to be; thus, he apologised and said that he had heard Magical Love talking to Mad Solo.

"So?" asked the Evil of Hate.

"So, I decided to shake things before Mad Solo would shake things. So, I recruited a male spider, who was on death row. I asked him to work for me in exchange for saving his life, for I thought if Mad Solo was helping Magical Love, then a SPIDER would fight from the evil side. I, however, and neither did the poor spider think that by escaping black widow's death row, he was about to get knocked by another black widow and change the course of the men of Wellingtonia."

"Unbelievable, Mr. Fate, what you are telling me is unimaginable," said the Evil of Hate.

"Believe me, it is beyond my belief too. But the only relief is that it would not help Phloxia in any way," said Mr. Fate hopefully.

"Hmm, I hope so and keep your involvement to the minimum; however, I'm not sure why it occurs to me that Phloxia has faulty genes or, say, defective genomes. Now that Queen Mother has a full-on dominant genome, I'm not sure why, even though they are totally unrelated, they still have something that feels like two and two, four. Making me think it is a coincidence or God Of Humanity's game?"

"Don't worry, evil friend, this love lot is doomed, no matter what plot the God Of Humanity has. I assure you that having the dominant genome only means more brutal conditions for Deutzo Hydrang's marriage," Mr. Fate explained.

"Hmm, but who would save the men of Wellingtonia from a woman with Spiderman's genes?" wondered the Evil of Hate.

"Mad Solo, there are talks that Mad Solo can help. He is a physicist," said Mr. Fate.

"A physicist? Never heard of one. I only know he was an amateur scientist," said the Evil of Hate, feeling bad.

"A physicist is a scientist, my evil friend," said Mr. Fate.

"Then call him a scientist," said the Evil of Hate, going back to his chair in the air, shaking his head in disbelief.

Mr. Fate went back to fulfil his lifelong mission to keep an eye on life on both lands, so as not to dwindle his focus.

Prince Deutzo now mostly spent his time in his room and would escape to the woods to find himself at night. He felt lost and needed someone's affection to give him confidence in life. However, it did not matter what he would do at night; he would spend the daytime with men around the lake. That environment would cheer him up, for did no matter what was going around, men were always in good spirits waiting for Mad Solo, the physicist, to come in action and save the men of Wellingtonia.

Unaware of all that, Ms Destiny slept, so as Phloxia slept thinking about her Prince and her life, decided to live a life as it flows.

Thus, the next day, Phloxia woke up before her mum, made tea, and decided to live a quiet life, one that would flow freely without any effort. However, it seemed to her that living that life was a kind of effort for her, and the one that she wanted to live would be rather effortless.

I need to adapt to the circumstances and conditions provided by the current reality. Once I have adapted, it will be effortless for me too. Fish have gills to breathe, humans have lungs, and frogs have both lungs and gills. I will be a frog in a couple of days, happy either way, doing what others ask me to do, and in my free time, as Villiea said, I can dream whatever I want. Only, I must make sure not to mix professional life with my personal life, and I am sure to handle that, for I am Phloxia D. Dron, with all the mutations a D. Dron could have.

She was thinking all this while her mother was drinking tea. "I told you to stop thinking, Phloxia, and you seem to have taken an oath not to listen to me."

"I was not thinking, Mother. I was planning how to spend my days."

"Hmm, that is a very good question. I will ask Yarrow Dron to arrange something for you. First, perhaps, he could arrange to send some ladies who are friendly here. You can talk to them supervised, and once you learn to talk to people, we will let you talk unsupervised to others."

"What?" Phloxia was confused.

"Dear Phloxia, when your sisters were here, you did not realise, but this is the way of life. People visit you, you visit them, and that is how life goes on."

"Whatever," said Phloxia. She went to her room, put all the books on the shelf, did some cleaning, had some food, and repeated the whole process the next day—not in that order, maybe, but something like that. And she did that every day until it was so habitual that she did it without thinking.

She did try to think sometimes, but soon, she realised that when you're thinking and it has no meaning, then you do not find pleasure in it. Rather, it becomes a wound that is open and looking into it, opens a channel of communication with the unknown world and people, and this would be enchanting if it was possible, and a laceration if you believe it to be untrue. Living with an open wound and a laceration is like cutting a piece of your own organs every day, while also living a life that is effortless for others but is taking all your energy, for you hate it so much that you think of nothing but how to get used to it, and thinking of getting used to it is like putting nails into your heart, and I don't know what you call an individual who has a wound, a laceration, and nails in the heart, but Phloxia was experiencing it. Thus, she decided to shut doors on thinking, dreams or anything that is not real. The reality, pleasing or unpleasing, is at least the truth.

Phloxia, thus, spent her days doing the same things, as did Abelia, and in no time, two years passed, and good news started to come.

First, Villiea had a daughter. Then Paulia had a son. Then Villiea had a son, and Paulia had a daughter.

One day, Phloxia was looking at the book cabinet without thinking, and she looked at a book that said on the cover: *'Whose life are you living? Yours or someone else's?'*

Phloxia did not want to give any attention to it, for she had decided to not give herself any pain. *I want to stay numb.*

However, she thought she might visit Villiea and Paulia for a change, and so she shared her idea with her mother, who agreed, for Phloxia had been a good child for two years now.

Phloxia barely went anywhere outside her home for two years, and during this time, she gained a good perspective towards life. She decided that living life without objecting to its authenticity with judgemental statements and going with the flow was a way to embrace eternity—eternity, where time has no application, for you are living in a timeless zone without keeping track of your whereabouts, under a roof with definite rules and regulations.

So, as soon as she stepped outside her home, she realised it was a whole new world. It seemed as if time had come back into existence, for it would matter if she did not get to her sister's home before dark. Time does have a value when you are timebound, Phloxia realised.

On the way, Phloxia stopped next to a river, for she wanted to look at the water that was going with the flow.

Phloxia looked at the little waves, and it seemed the water and waves were very happy. That made Phloxia question her theory about going with the flow in life. *These waves are going with the flow and seem so happy, so if I am going with the flow, then why am I unhappy?* And that question undercut her ideology of happiness. *I am supposed to be jumping with joy, in the river of life, as this water is in the river of waves.* And then she had a Eureka moment. *I am not flowing. I am stagnant. I am not moving. Rather, I am stuck in the mud without any way out. I thought that this was my choice, but I am just the mud's toy.*

That thought changed her whole character in a moment. *I will never be happy if I don't shake things up. But how?*

However, she was timebound and had no time to answer her own questions, so she first went to meet Villiea, who she had last visited two years ago, when she had found her fairly dissatisfied, but to her amazement, today, she was exploding with *jouissance*.

"Oh, so you have adapted?" asked Phloxia.

"Having kids is like being in touch with your other self, Phloxia. I hope you find someone soon too."

I am thinking to shake things up a bit, and Villiea is thinking to bind me with wires so that it will be impossible to escape.

Anyhow, as Phloxia observed, it was a happy family, with two kids, one husband, and in-laws.

At the end of the day, as long as you are happy, that is all that matters.

The next day, Phloxia went to see Paulia. Paulia was incredibly joyous. She had a few financial worries here and there, but nothing big enough to cover the smiles that arose every morning like a sunrise after looking at two cute kids, a husband and everyone else.

Wow. Phloxia was satisfied with the general inference that whatever makes you happy is worth having.

On the way back, she thought of shaking things up. *No, I do not need to anymore,* she thought.

Staying stagnant is a happy life.

She looked at the river again, and there was a frog. *I was* supposed to be a frog with both gills and lungs, and it seems I have lost both and am now gasping for air, which will continue until I die. That sudden thought of death put the image of her dying father in her brain, which made her question her existence. That big question enlightened her fused electric globes, aka brain, by joining the filament of her thoughts. The electric force powered by her thoughts enlightened her soul; it was like the onset of a momentary thunderstorm or the struggle to take a breath just before death. Her thoughts were no longer dormant. As soon as she allowed her thoughts to flow freely in her nervous system, a feeling of immense power took her over.

Oh god, I am an idiot. What have I done to myself? What am I thinking? It is not accurate. There has to be more to life. I have been acting in a way that has been forced on me by a society that is too scared to accept anything that is not its own reflection. My mother wants to see her own image in me, and that, I am not, for reasons unknown to me, and trying to become that would only kill me slowly because changing your genetic makeup is impossible. Environmental factors do influence your character but cannot make you something you are not.

Whatever happens, I am going to make sure I am happy for as long as I am alive. That is that, and that is the way to shake things up. I mean, it is not that I am giving up on royal title; it is only the D. Drons who are short of money anyway.

While absorbed in these thoughts, she arrived home, where a big surprise was waiting for her with open arms.

Her mother came running to her, saying, "Get ready for the big day, darling. There is big news for you."

Phloxia suspected what the news might be considering the D. Drons associated the word 'big' with an occasion that might or might not be big itself but brings a big change in one's life and involves moving out of home and into a different residence; she'd just had a spiritual awakening on her way back home after looking at a frog that reminded her of her dead self instead of a prince, which frogs are usually associated with.

Okay, that was all, she said to her mother, which perplexed her.

Abelia also had an instant feeling of fear that the old Phloxia with faulty genes was back. She gave Phloxia a suspicious look and asked what had happened.

"Nothing," Phloxia replied and went to the bookshelf, which had been untouched for two years, give or take a week.

"Something must have happened, for you had stopped reading books," her mother insisted.

Phloxia shook her head. She took a random book and sat in a chair.

"Well, Phloxia, you have been behaving perfectly for two years, so I will be straight with you. They are coming tomorrow to talk to you, and make sure nothing you do displays your true character to strangers."

"Hmm," said Phloxia as she realised the book's title was '*Hidden Ways of Finding Freedom*'.

The irony is that she smiled and started reading to get some tips before facing a situation that did not make her at all nervous. It was as if her fear had been taken by her mother, who was looking at her anxiously while waiting for Yarrow to come and discuss the developing situation.

While waiting for Yarrow to come, her mother asked her to make tea instead of wasting her eyesight on something irrelevant to her way of life, for D. Drons find freedom in following the thousand-year-old rituals, which no one knew the origin of but everyone claimed to know the importance of, for these traditions were in their blood.

Phloxia made tea, and by now, she knew how to make tea properly. She and her mother sat drinking tea, and there came Yarrow. Phloxia got up and gave tea to her uncle too.

Abelia looked at Phloxia as if to ask her to continue reading the book but without letting it alter anything in her brain. She wanted to discuss an important issue with Yarrow Dron.

Phloxia wanted that too. So, she sat at a distance close enough to listen to the conversation between her mother and uncle while pretending to read.

"You do not need to say anything, Abelia," started Yarrow. "I know everything, for some people saw Phloxia wandering around the river that comes from nowhere and goes nowhere. It is a never-ending river. The river tends to make people think about their faults, for it is a perfect example of eternal life. It is not living, will not die, and it flows continuously without visible end."

"I heard that the river ends near to where I am from, Yarrow," said Abelia, to disclose another secret.

"Hmm, that is why I said no visible end."

"So, what is the solution now? Tomorrow, the big party is coming to see her, and if they see her like she is now, her big day will never come."

"There is a man who knows the nostrum for screwy people."

"A man? Can we trust him completely?" asked Abelia, for she was worried such a man could screw up Phloxia even more.

"Trust me; this man knows what he is doing. He is known as a 'crystal gazer', for that is the work he does. He looks into his crystal, which shows the solution for the nostrum according to the condition, and he can identify the condition by just looking at the person. Tomorrow morning, we will take her to this future-teller."

"What about the arrival of the big party?" asked Abelia, looking worried.

"I will ask the big party to delay Phloxia's fluctuating wedding date by another day," said Yarrow.

Yarrow was visibly irritated by all this, for finding a husband seemed harder to him than finding anything else. He could imagine himself writing a book on the 'hidden tricks of finding a husband' for dear little, screwed-up Phloxia, and his book would be heavier and more extensive than the one Phloxia was holding, which was about hidden ways of finding freedom. Yarrow knew from experience that the more books weigh, the more they are worth. He had been selling books to recycling stations without anyone's knowledge, so he knew what he was talking about.

When Yarrow left, Abelia went to the village to see if the news of her daughter was thought to be only a rumour among people or had been confirmed to be accurate by someone. If the latter scenario applied, she would have to devise ways to debunk the whole story as nothing but an attention-seeking activity by someone who was not given any attention by anyone alive.

While this scene of love and hate for the D. Drons unfolded, Ms Destiny was watching behind closed doors, for she had left her invisible cloak at home as the weather was too hot. Also, she had a slight feeling that Magical Love might also be keeping an eye on the whole situation; since he had escorted her home, Ms Destiny has developed a little fondness for him.

Future-teller? said Ms Destiny to herself. *A future-teller, if appropriately used, can do wonders for someone and turn around their path to escape fate and help them reach their destiny. So, he* might be my man to drive Phloxia overly crazy, then harness her hidden powers to land her in the land of Wellingtonia, where it would be straightforward to bring the two lovebirds together.

So, Ms Destiny disguised herself as a random woman from the village and went straight home to pick up her cloak, for the sun was about to set, and a cool breeze was blowing, which was bringing down the temperature. Also, she knew that this future-teller only had one door, mainly closed, to not allow people from inside to leave without paying for his services rendered. That meant she would have nowhere to hide while planning and transferring her vision to the future-teller.

When she got to the future-teller, he was fast asleep, and the door was open. *Wasted my time picking up my cloak,* she thought, but then put it on to wake him up by scaring him to his soul, for she needed his eyes open when transferring her vision to him.

As she moved closer to wake the future-teller, the door suddenly closed, and the sound of it closing scared her to her soul.

She looked back, and there was Magical Love, without any cloak on, looking at her without moving his eyes.

"Why are you here?" asked Ms Destiny, putting her hand on her heart, which was still throbbing from the sound of the old door, which was like the door of an old, abandoned container in an old yard that pregnant cats use to sleep in at night to be safe from mad dogs that would, instead, wander in abandoned sheds. "I have to tell you something."

"Tell me after; wait for me outside," said Ms Destiny.

"No, I need to talk to you right now; right now is too late even. I should have already told you by now." Magical Love was hysterical.

"Come in my cloak and tell me what is so urgent that you

are breathing heavily enough to wake up this old future-teller, who would not otherwise wake up from the sound of a train or his slamming door."

As soon as Magical Love put his head in the cloak, he could not even hear, but he could see Ms Destiny's beautiful soft skin with tiny clothes on.

Magical Love looked at her with love. His eyes were filled with mixed emotions and his feet were moving uncontrollably. The turbulence resulted in him accidentally putting his right foot on Ms Destiny's left foot high heel. The discomfort activated Ms Destiny's automatic reflexes, and she nailed Magical Love's left foot with her right foot's sharp heel. Now they were both in pain, and they escaped outside so they could freely yell at each other.

They yelled and yelled until both parties realised they had forgotten the primary mission and were beating around the bush, which was the only thing in the yard except the abandoned container.

"We should go to a safer place before pregnant cats come here to have a good night's sleep," said Magical Love.
"Agreed," said Ms Destiny with a nod. "Let's go to my place."
As Ms Destiny settled down a little, she shot the first question. "What?"

Magical Love looked at her and repeated the question. "What?"

"Why did you barge in, when I was trying to do something productive?" asked Ms Destiny.

"Oh, I had to tell you something, but it is probably too late already, so I might tell you about the new developing situation."

"What?" asked Ms Destiny, for she was confused and irritated. She realised that Magical Love was going to continue this conversation for longer than usual, so she sat on her comfortable sofa.

"Take your time," said Ms Destiny, getting comfortable in her seat.

"No, no, I will not take too long. I want to say that it seems as if I am in love."

"What? You are not in love; you are Magical Love."

"Oh no, Ms Destiny. I am in love with you. I have been since I saw your beautiful skin and sense of fashion that you like to put tiny clothes on. My emotions are unstoppably desiring your sweet company forever."

"Ha, my sweet company! You mad dog, as if you don't know how much I like savoury food."

"I don't care what you call me or what you eat. All I care about is that your throbbing heart has caused me throbbing pain, and only sweet death or your soft, butter-like touch can make my life a dream, a dream that I was always too scared to see, for seeing another fail in their dreams filled me with much fear, but, magically, the vision of your hammering bosom took all my fear away, and I am left with nothing but thoughts of wanting what I have seen."

"Oh, what I hear is an attraction to what you have seen, and that has nothing to do with love," declared Ms Destiny.

"Believe me, sweet pea. I am the Magical Love, and no one knows more than I do about love."

"Oh, if that is love, then why is Phloxia falling for someone in her dreams ?"

"Oh, that is different. Love, darling, may I?" asked Magical Love, getting permission to sit close to Ms Destiny, as if the story was going to take a while to tell. As Magical Love sat down right next to Ms Destiny, he said, "You missed the point at the very beginning of this set-up. What Phloxia is experiencing is called twin flame love. And my brother, my younger brother, is taking care of another lovebird, Deutzo Hydrang. That was what I was about to tell you when you invited me under the cloak, and I forgot everything I was supposed to say."

"Your brother? I did not know you had a brother," Ms Destiny said, blinking her eyelids fast, as if proud of her beauty.

"Will you have dinner with me tonight?" asked Magical Love.

"What? Tell me about your brother first."

"His name is Mr T. Flame. His services are usually free, for people do not care much about him that much, and I am the popular one," said Magical Love proudly. "However, in this case, I needed his expertise, but because he was not part of our group when the bet was set up, I had to bribe him to work for me."

"Oh." Ms Destiny was surprised. "I thought you wanted an easy win. Then why did you use the love potion on Cyclamen?"

"Hmm, that is what everyone thinks, but those two lovebirds… There was a reason that they took our attention. We are extra-terrestrial. Still, we were attracted to the display of affection the two birds were showing, and the reason was that they were not two, but one. To put it simply, twin flame love is one soul split into two. Those birds had one soul, and now so do Phloxia and the Deutzo Hydrang, our other lovebird."

"What does that mean?" asked Ms Destiny, getting up to make some popcorn, for she loved having popcorn if the story was interesting.

"That means, unless they kill their inner conflict, as Phloxia did for two years, they will not be happy or satisfied."

"Hmm, interesting. Why do you care, though? And it still does not explain your love potion use," Ms Destiny said, sitting again and passing popcorn to Magical Love.

"I like ice cream," said Magical Love.

"Don't have any," said Ms Destiny and, instead, gave him a cold drink. She put some whisky in it without telling Magical Love, for she wanted him to vomit up the story quickly so she could plan her next steps.

After having a cold drink, Magical Love started talking faster than a parrot. "I was about to take a wrong turn. I thought making Phloxia fall in love and winning the bet would be enough, but it is not. I realised that after seeing you under the cloak. Love has to be honest and pure. You have changed my whole character. I am in love with you. I am Magical Love. But the bad news is that on the other side of this land, Deutzo Hydrang is struggling with his emotions and trying to fall in love without success. He is lucky, though, to have no restriction on having relations, so whether it is love or not doesn't matter that much unless he is in the meadow with his shadow."

"However, my brother, T Flame, said that if he marries, it will be difficult for him to end the relationship. He is very kind and caring. Queen Mother is looking for a suitable match, which is a woman with all dominant genes. My brother will try to delay things, but I am not sure for how long. It is necessary for Phloxia to get to the land of Wellingtonia as soon as possible. It might be difficult for them to meet, but at least there would be some hope. Here, there is no hope, no hope at all, no hope… Would you go out for dinner with me tonight?" At this point, Magical Love was sleep-talking.

"Hmm, love is drunk, not blind," said Destiny and laughed as she got ready to sleep too.

She wasn't sure how long she slept for, but suddenly, she heard strange voices in the kitchen, and she thought it might be Love, but then she looked around and saw Magical Love was still asleep next to her.

Ms Destiny was scared and wanted to wake up Magical Love, but if he hadn't woken up already from the sound of the beating drums in the kitchen, then it would be a waste of time trying to get his help.

So Ms Destiny went to her jewellery room to get her courage. Ms Destiny liked to wear this piece of jewellery in the dark, for it was shiny and could be seen even in darkness. "I like this brand," said Ms Destiny to herself. "Courage. I feel courageous when wearing it."

So now that Ms Destiny had courage around her neck, she entered the kitchen, and there they were. *I knew it; they must have followed me home from around the bush.*

Two pregnant cats, looking for food.

Ms Destiny gave them some extra food for the mad dog too in case he saw them on the way, and then she let them go.

The pregnant cats looked at the sleeping Magical Love and laughed on their way out. They didn't say anything but were certainly thinking about their nights of love.

Ms Destiny put her courage back in its case and went to sleep again. Again, she was not sure how long she was asleep for before she heard beating drums again in the kitchen.

"Oh god," she said.

Then a reply came. "No, no, it is not God, my love. It's me, your Magical Love."

"Why are you awake so late?" asked Ms Destiny.

"Oh, that cold drink was very strong. I slept before telling you my whole plan. We need to shake things up before tomorrow's sunrise, for I want to come back and sleep in. I like sleeping in and don't mind working till late," said Magical Love casually.

"I prefer to wake up early and sleep early," said Ms Destiny, and put her head down to go back to sleep.

"No, you don't, Ms Destiny. For now, I am thinking about you more than me."

"Can't you shake things up yourself? For if you had not ruined things when I was about to shake things up, then we would not be having this talk."

"Well, you know why all that happened, for you shook me up. I am still shaking. It is too cold."

"Here, I'll put some music on," said Magical Love, trying to move around and look for music.

"You are cold and looking for music? I have a heater," said Ms Destiny.

"Let's dance and warm up before leaving." Magical Love pulled Ms Destiny off her bed.

"Are you serious, Magical Love?"

"Just call me Love," said Magical Love, smiling.

"Anyhow, do I need my cloak?" asked Ms Destiny.

"No need; it is dark outside."

"What is the plan?" asked Ms Destiny.

"I have arranged a meeting for tomorrow morning with The God of Humanity, for whatever is happening, it renders it impossible for us to win. We have to shake things up at the D. Dron house first. Phloxia is our prime target."

"You are confusing me."

"Hmm, some things we can control and others we can't. Falling in love with you, for example, I could not control, but you are showing great self-control there. So, Phloxia's marriage to this new man might be inevitable, but that should not stop her from dreaming, so while you are shaking things up, I will mix my love potion made of dreams, and dreams only, in her water that Mr Strained Eyes told me she has first thing every morning to keep her beauty intact."

"Mr Strained Eyes?"

"Oh, yes, you don't know. We call Mr Fate 'Strained Eyes' in our friend circle. You have been too proud to join."

"What do you mean? No one ever asked me." Ms Destiny was not happy to hear that.

"Well, we assumed that anyway."

"Whatever," said Ms Destiny. "Anyhow, where is Mr Fate? I mean, what if he is watching us doing all this and is playing his games without us knowing?" asked Ms Destiny. She was now holding her heels in her hands, for it was difficult for her to keep up with Magical Love.

"I am happy to carry you in my arms," said Magical Love with a smile before he went on. "And Mr Fate has decided to go to the land of Wellingtonia to follow my brother to make sure Mr T. Flame does not shake things up for him."

"Really?" Ms Destiny asked in disbelief.

"Only for a week or two, for he did not see any imminent change in circumstances happening, so it is the best time for us to shake things up."

While engaging in this light talk, they got to the D. Dron residence.

"Well, it is a good thing that it is dark, so I do not need to shake things up," said Ms Destiny, feeling relieved.

"Why? We always need to shake things up," said Magical Love.

"But it is dark; we don't need to distract their attention, so you could mix the dream potion in her drink."

"Oh, so, you don't know, Ms Destiny? I don't get someone to shake things up to divert anyone's anything. I don't need that."

"Then why?" Ms Destiny was impatient now.

"My love potion does not work without shaking things up. It is for that." Magical Love was serious.

Ms Destiny shook her head first, then the nearby tree, while Magical Love mixed the love potion. He put mostly dreams into it and put it in the glass of water next to Phloxia's bed.

As the tree was shaken, a momentary storm came, and that woke Abelia, and she ran out, thinking it was Phloxia gone completely mental.

Ms Destiny and Magical Love took shelter in the dark shadows before leaving to go and see the crystal gazer.

"What are you going to do when we get there?" asked Ms Destiny.

"I have a love potion with mostly a psychic element in it. I am going to mix it with his drinks."

"All of them?"

"That is what I have been thinking. Then my sources told me that the milk he has in his fridge, he uses in the morning to have tea. So this love potion is going in his milk. After drinking the milk, he is going to gain insight into Phloxia's past and she will tell him the whole story." As Magical Love said this, he showed Ms Destiny a strange powder. "That is what you wanted too?" asked Magical Love, looking at Ms Destiny. "I am doing it for you," he said, looking at her beautiful black mini dress. "You are a beautiful woman, Ms Destiny. I never realised that before today. I always found you a little on the tough side as a woman, but I was wrong. You are quite the woman to tame my heart."

"Don't start stories; mix it," said Ms Destiny, who wanted to go back home and sleep.

"I cannot; you have to go and shake things first."

"It is a city, and I do not see any trees around," said Ms Destiny sleepily.

"What about that bush we were beating around earlier?"

"Do you want me to go there now? What about the pregnant cats?"

"They will be in a deep sleep by now; it is quite late, almost four." Magical Love signalled for Ms Destiny to hurry.

"People wake up at four, Magical Love. It is early, not late," said Ms Destiny, almost cursing her fate.

"Sane people don't wake up that early," said Magical Love. "Nor do ones not in love," he said, looking at Ms Destiny meaningfully before she walked over to shake the bush.

As soon as the bush was shaking, Magical Love mixed the love potion, containing ninety-nine per cent 'psychic', into the milk.

Magical Love and Ms Destiny walked back home.

"Mission achieved, and now we can sleep," Magical Love said and went straight to bed.

"I might sleep a bit more too. Oh, but I am going to check if the cats followed me."

She looked around, and it was all clear, with no sign of any invasion by cats, so Ms Destiny went to sleep.

So, it was a new day, and almost eleven. Ms Destiny woke up Magical Love and asked him if he wanted to have coffee.

Magical Love loved to have coffee and nodded.

"Go and make one for me too," said Ms Destiny and settled down on her comfortable couch.

Magical Love could not say no, for she was his first love. He had seen many passions unfold before but had fallen himself for the first time.

The coffee was served in the invisible cups, and as they sat drinking, someone knocked on the door.

Who could there be? both Magical Love and Ms Destiny thought.

The best way to find out who is at a door is to go and check, and Magical Love, of course, did go and check, for being in love means you are ready to do anything for that special someone of yours.

"Oh, this is the newspaper," Magical Love said, looking at the main headline: *'Two feral cats knocked the daylight out of a wild dog, who was chasing them under cover of darkness.'*

"How did that happen?" Magical Love was befuddled by the dramatic nature of the news.

"Oh, I know," Ms Destiny said casually. "I gave two cats some food, thinking they were from the bush we were beating around earlier."

"Food? It still does not explain their uncivilised behaviour."

"Well, I had spilled whisky everywhere earlier. On food, in drinks—you name it."

"Hmm." Magical Love thought for a minute. "That explains my sudden passing out too."

"Yes," replied Ms Destiny, drinking invisible coffee from invisible cups. "So, when are we starting to put your plan into action?" Ms Destiny finished her invisible tea from the invisible cup.

"What plan? Remind me?" said a confused Magical Love.

"Last night, remember, we mixed your magic potion into drinks, and you said we would meet The God of Humanity today?"

"Ah," Magical Love looked at his watch. "It is too late to see The God of Humanity. We will have to arrange it for another day. Wake me earlier next time, dear."

"Hey, Magical Love, I allowed your not-so-magical advances last night, for you were out of your mind after having one drink. I am not your girlfriend. Let me know if there is anything you have on your mind before wasting my time by not using your brain and trying to confuse me more than I already am. I am losing my race here, and you are talking to me about love, when the love you are supposed to save is dwindling. You are favouring those who will win, when Phloxia and Deutzo Hydrang's story is dissolving in your magic potion and will never regain its physical state ever."

"Aha, you can talk. And thanks for reminding me of my magic potion. Let's check the ramifications. We will head first to see the D. Drons to find out how Phloxia is tracking. She will be, by now, completely under my influence. She will be like me. She will sound like me, and eat like me." Magical Love was confident.

"And how would that help us?" asked Ms Destiny.

"Well, you don't know the success stories, it seems, Ms Destiny, which makes sense to me now. Why do you fear being overthrown by all of us? Would you please allow me to rouse your soul with my very eye-opening success story? In fact, let's call it 'success story number one'. It has turned me into who I am today. confident, creative and conqueror: **three magical c's have followed me wherever I go since then.**"

Ms Destiny was thinking of Magical Love as being 'careless', so she volunteered to hear his 'three magical c's success story number one', and it was a good way to pass time on the way to see the D. Drons.

"So, it is the story of when I was about seventeen, around Phloxia's age. I used to think of myself as Romeo, for, without my knowledge, I was filled with love. At that tender age, Ms Destiny, I was on the lookout for my Juliet."

"Oh," reacted Ms Destiny.

"I know it might be a bit of a touchy subject for you, considering our flame has been recently ignited."

"I am all right; you go on."

"Now, you might not know, but I was born into a huge family and had all kinds of relations, starting from my mother and taking it back to early man, the man who discovered how to make fire. There it started, and our family were famous for discoveries and inventions. I wanted to continue this noble profession of discovering something not already in existence by finding a woman so enchanting, so perfect, that it would be hard to believe that she existed."

"Two years passed without any success, for finding someone so unreal and non-existent was a real challenge, and then I came into contact with this person who called himself 'The D.'."

"The D?" repeated Ms Destiny.

"Hmm, The D. and I became friends, for both of us shared a common interest in women; the only difference was that he would go for any, and I was looking for the unreal one. Then he told me the secret of tracing the source of one's thirstiness. This is precisely what he said, 'When you lie under a tree, wander around the world in your flight of fancy, sipping on your own choice of drink; wherever it takes you is the place you need to be to retrieve the gold you seek'."

"I took him seriously, for he was unique. I went home and was fortunate to have a tree in my backyard. I followed his instructions and lay under the tree and, in my thoughts, wandered to a new location while sipping on my tea."

"Later, I realised it was not so tricky, for the location it took me to was a pub that was behind that abandoned container where we were beating around last night. I was not allowed to visit anywhere hidden, and, thus, I explained my problem to him."

"The D. was very sensible when it came to his words, so if he said that wherever my flight of fancy took me would be the right location, he meant it. So, he then gave me the solution and taught me the recipe of the magic potion after I insisted. Anyhow, he gave me the magic potion called 'magic concupiscence', and it was made from—not ten, twenty or fifty—that potion was a hundred per cent made of the fourth c (concupiscence); that is the secret that makes the other three c's follow me."

"As soon as I had it dissolved in my choice of drink, I found myself totally in another world, and no one could stop me from doing or getting what I wanted; I went straight to the bar behind the abandoned container, had a couple more drinks, and there she was my 'Moggie'. I had found what I wanted, a beauty so unreal that it could not exist. Although I had a fantastic night with her, the next day, she vanished."

"Vanished?" asked Ms Destiny.

"Hmm, vanished into the abandoned container where she slept during the day and that pregnant cats used at night. That is the story of my first real goal and accomplishment. From then on, anything I have desired has come true, so by now, Phloxia, under the influence of 'magic concupiscence', would have started to invent ways to get what she really wants." "Interesting," said Ms Destiny. "But Moggie? I thought you said last night that I was your first love?"

"True love—you are my first true love. I first met Moggie in a flight of fancy, so she was 'in-flight love', and you are 'in-cloak love'."

"God," said Ms Destiny, who was a little unimpressed by his story.

"You can tell an interesting story if you like; there is still some distance to go."

"My story might not be as pleasing as yours, for it does not have a happy ending. Anyhow, I was about nineteen, more like Deutzo's age. I saw this man, so young and good-looking that I could not believe my eyes."

"In a flight of fancy?" asked Magical Love.

"Oh, no, around my house where I live now. So, I decided to find out how to talk to him and where to meet him, and then my source told me that he goes to a pub every evening."

"Behind the abandoned container?" asked Magical Love.

"No, behind the abandoned barn, the one that mad dogs use for whatever. I always lived by myself but was still scared of such a bar behind an abandoned barn. I knew one of my friends, 'Moxie', knew something that would make you do the impossible, so I went to visit him. I told him the problem, and as I said, he knew what he was talking about, so he said, 'Why don't you take a doggo with you?' For I was scared to go there alone, and a doggo would give me company and could enjoy the company of the mad dogs while we were there."

"Oh, so that is how you met your man?"

"No, I never met him, and for a fascinating reason, which the crystal gazer told me on the way back home. He said that man was visiting me in his flight of fancy, and that is how I saw him."

"It did not make any sense until you told me your story. I am sure he visited me in a flight of fancy but did not know how to get to me, for he would not have known your friend, The D., who could have shown him the way to make it possible, to land the flight and not just stay in a flight of fancy."

"Hmm, sorrowful story. A real sad one. Could you please pass me some tissues?" asked Magical Love, who had a runny nose, for the wind was cold and the sun was hiding under the dark clouds, which were there to make the day of dark stories about the past even darker. "But you get the gist of what I am talking about. We all know that Phloxia has seen him in her flight of fancy or is a creation of her brain or whatever you call it. She likes what she sees and does feel attracted to him, as she described him as a magnet—'her magnet', to be precise."

"What is she missing? She is missing someone to show her how to get what she wants. My drink, which is made of the fourth c, invented by the D., would show her dream man the trail to her. In fact, by now, she would be on her way to her port of call."

"Hmm, I did not think that you did extensive planning. I had assumed that it was just another drink, like the one you used for Cyclamen D. Manhood for brief arousal."

"Ha-ha-ha," laughed Magical Love for as long as he could, holding onto his stomach. He said, 'Poor Cyclamen. He would not be able to explain his own behaviour to himself, let alone anyone else. One-third of that magical potion was love.'

"Its effects wore off quite quickly, though," said Ms Destiny.

"It is not that its effects wore off. He was still under its influence when he got married, for he was marrying someone else and thinking about Phloxia."

"You are clever," said Ms Destiny.
"I'll take that as a compliment," said Magical Love.
"What did you have in the crystal gazer's milk?" Ms Destiny wanted to know it all.

"Seventeen per cent insight into the future and thirty per cent psychic ability. Well, we are almost at the D. Dron residence.

Let's sit and have some rest, for who knows what we are going to face there. By now, Phloxia might have started walking on her path by plotting the plan on a piece of paper, writing everything in detail on it. So, under the influence of my magic potion, this future-teller would tell her how to achieve the plot drawn on the paper under the influence of my drug."

"Oh," said Ms Destiny.

"That is how I do things. I make sure to match the intensity of my goal with my actions, and that is how I make sure to have three c's following me everywhere. From now on, one D too," Magical Love said, looking at Ms Destiny, who seemed impressed by his plan. "So, tell me, woman of my dreams, what do you think?"

"Oh, I do think the plan is excellent, and it might work."

"Don't worry about the plan. The plan was sure to work as soon as I planned it. That is how I do things and make the three c's follow me. I know what works and how it works. Now that I am in your life, you do not have to worry about anything. I will plan everything. So I will repeat my question. What do you think?" asked Magical Love, showing her two tickets for the movie *Hidden Ways of Dating a Strong-willed Woman.*

"It is not a movie," said Ms Destiny, laughing.

"Not yet maybe, but there will be one after today. You will start dating me because you are so impressed by me; I can tell from your happy and unworried face."

"I am impressed, for sure."

"So, there is a movie, for the movie was made when I decided to create one."

They laughed and then laughed some more before heading off to see the D. Drons. Just as they arrived, they saw Yarrow going in.

"Did you bring your invisible cloak?" asked Magical Love.

"Oh, I did, but look at Abelia. What is going on here?" asked Ms Destiny.

There was a strange scene unfolding. Abelia, Phloxia's mother, had a couple of pieces of paper in front of her, and she was drawing something on them.

Phloxia and Yarrow Dron were standing around and looking at her, while Magical Love and Ms Destiny were also observing from under their cloak, with their eyes on the pieces of paper and the drawings on them.

"Mother has been doing it all morning: drawing, then putting the piece of paper in the bin, then pulling it out again, and talking to me strangely. It seems something has happened to Mother."

"Something has happened?" But then Yarrow Dron asked, "What did you eat last night? Did someone give you something, or did your mother go and see someone?"

"No, nothing like that happened. I slept in my room, and Mother woke up this morning and made tea for me, saying something strange."

"What did she say?" asked a visibly upset Yarrow.

"Mother said that life comes only once and is very short, so she should plan something that will not take very long."

"That does not make any sense," said Yarrow.

"I know," replied Phloxia.

"Abelia, are you all right? Do you want to have tea?" asked Yarrow Dron.

"Oh, Yarrow. I did not realise you were here. Sure. My dear child, Phloxia, go and make some tea for all of us."

"What are you drawing?" asked Yarrow Dron.

"Oh, it is nothing. I always wanted to have a new kitchen, and, suddenly, I feel like I can do it myself, for the D. Drons are short of money. I have found a way to help me renovate the kitchen, and it will not take very long. Come, and I will show you," said Abelia, moving the piece of paper towards Yarrow Dron.

"I will start soon after the design is complete, and then it will take me about a month to get it ready. I might ask Cornus D. Homo Sapien and Darmar to help me, and that will quicken the process. In no time, we will have a new kitchen. How does that sound to you?" Abelia asked Yarrow Dron.

And while saying that, Abelia had started to make some corrections and changes on the pieces of paper.

"Are you sure nothing else happened, Phloxia?" asked Yarrow Dron again.

"Oh, yes. I remember. At about two or three in the morning, Mother heard our tree shaking and came out to check, but no one was out there," Phloxia said, pointing at the tree. "Then Mother came to my room and was very scared because the tree was still shaking, but no one was there. Mother was so terrified that she drank one full glass of water from next to my bed. Then she went back to sleep and, since she woke up, has been doing tasks that are inexplicable to me. Mother has been talking to me with a great deal of love, though, and I like that."

While that conversation was going on, Ms Destiny looked at Magical Love and almost threw him out of the cloak.

"That is your plan?" she said, pointing at Abelia. "Plotting a way to her port of call, which is a new kitchen? Now, explain to me where are your three c's: confidence, contempt and conquest? Have they not followed you here today?"

"I did not know that Abelia would be scared of a mere tree shaking to the extent that she would drink a whole lot of water prepared specially for Phloxia."

"What will happen now?"

"She will make sure to complete her kitchen, and I will have to prepare another drink by sourcing all the ingredients worldwide. I better go and get it ready, for I sense we will need it sooner rather than later. You stay here and keep an eye on things and keep me updated."

"That's strange," said Ms Destiny.

"The D. Drons are getting a new kitchen. It is all right. It is not the first time this has happened to me. I have seen it before, and the consequences have always been positive. I will be back." And with that said, Magical Love left, and Ms Destiny watched Abelia draw things on a piece of paper.

"We were supposed to go to the future-teller today." Yarrow Dron looked at Abelia.

"Oh, Yarrow. I know how much you care about dear Phloxia. You see, I am swamped today, and it seems like the next two months are going to be bustling, so why don't you take her to the future-teller yourself? Also, I do not know the future-teller, so he would be more comfortable with you."

Yarrow Dron looked at Phloxia.

"Mother needs help. Something has happened to her, it seems. What about we take her to the psychic too?"

"It seems someone is here who is not letting things happen," said Yarrow Dron, looking around.

Ms Destiny checked her cloak to make sure she was not visible, for it seemed as if Yarrow could sense her presence.

"The future-teller's name is Augur. He is outstanding when it comes to looking at the house and seeing what we cannot see. What about we get him here instead, and he looks around, looks at Abelia, and then at you too? That would solve all of our issues.

I ignored your mother when she said that a roaring crow was a bad sign, but it seems she was right. It is good you are not married to Cyclamen."

Phloxia looked at her uncle and thought, *It seems Augur would need to look at him too. I mean, where is this whole story going? Mother only wants a new kitchen, and she is determined now.*

Anyhow, she only said, "Do anything that seems right to you, Uncle."

Her uncle left to get the future-teller.

Phloxia had free time, and her mum was busy doing her own thing, so she looked at a book, *Hidden in Your Backyard*, and started reading while Ms Destiny watched from under her cloak.

You know what you see, and there might be things that you do not see, or things that you see but are not there. Look around. Do you feel something? Feelings are all right, for feelings come from inside; they have nothing to do with the outside.

You live in a house and have a backyard; you are worried about it, aren't you? You are a soul, and your body is your backyard. Have you ever tried to look into it and see yourself or something you are hiding from yourself? Are you the real you? Or is there more to you?

I cannot answer your questions. Only you can. This book is not about what is out there. Don't worry about what is out there, for if something or someone wants to be in touch with you, it will be through your soul, your spirit. So, worry about your inside vision. Worry about the real you. Once that happens, you will see what you desire to see. You will see what you feel, for what you feel will show you both the inside and outside.

When you look at a tree, the one in your backyard, try to smile at it, and it will smile back at you. It is about acceptance.

Accept your inner self, and your surroundings will accept you.

There is a little exercise I want you to do for a week. Anything that you notice or see that comes from within, give it your full attention and try to understand its language. Then keep giving it your attention unless you do not like it, and if you do not want it, then find some other seed inside your backyard, one you like, and then grow it in your backyard, both inside and outside.

"Oh, that is heavy," said Phloxia. "I might have to reread it." Then she started to read the words out to herself but loudly.

"Oh, dear Phloxia. You do not have to reread it. You have to accept what you are reading," said Abelia.

"Strange," said Ms Destiny from under the cloak.

Phloxia made some more tea and sat in the backyard, looking at the tree. She tried to smile, and it seemed to her, even in the quietness of the afternoon, that the tree shook a little to smile back at her.

"Hidden in your backyard," she said. "I mean, that is right. Even though someone is sitting right beside me, there is nothing that I can do."

"Yes, right," said Ms Destiny from under the cloak.

"I do have something in the backyard inside me. Yes, I do, and I see someone and like them too. But how can I grow that seed in my backyard when I might be getting married very soon?"

"Oh, don't worry, Phloxia. Magical Love has gone to make another love potion," said Ms Destiny from under the cloak.

Phloxia closed her eyes to see what she had forgotten or wanted to forget, but in your backyard, you can ignore something but you cannot forget it. Ignoring something does not make it disappear, and it appears as soon as your vision settles on it again. That is exactly what happened to Phloxia as she closed her eyes; there he was, the best-looking man in this whole world—for her, at least.

"Who are you?" she asked. "Why do I see you? Where are you? How do I get to you?"

"Well, the crystal gazer will answer those questions hopefully. Magical Love needs to come back in time with a new magic potion of the fourth c or Augur's talk will not make sense to you nor yours to Augur, the future-teller." Ms Destiny kept talking from under her cloak without anyone noticing.

Phloxia had her own answers, and then they heard a knock on the door. There they were, both of her sisters. Their uncle had called them in to support Phloxia while Abelia was working on her new kitchen with a dedication that required results.

"Oh, Phloxia, what happened?" asked both Paulia and Villiea.

"Something terrible has happened," said Phloxia. "Mother drank a glass full of water last night and is still affected by it."

"Oh, that is bad. Our mother is on water, and you are on faulty genes, and we have something in the backyard," said Villiea.

Ms Destiny, standing in the backyard under the cloak, said, "What is wrong with the D. Drons? They are putting my whole existence in limbo."

"No, Villiea. Nothing is out there; everything is in here, right here in our backyard," said Phloxia, pointing towards her heart.

"What are you on now?" asked Paulia, who was scared by the conversation between her sisters. "It does not matter whether it is out there or in here. It is scary and should not be mentioned. If we talk about it, we might be in danger. I have heard stories about a thing that abducts whoever says its name."

"Who are you talking about?" asked Villiea.

"Rocko, the famous thief, who quickly gets to any backyard and does not need keys to get in anywhere."

"No, I was talking about ghosts," said Villiea.

"And I was talking about spirits," said Phloxia.

"Hmm, ghosts, spirits and thieves are all so alike; they tend not to be seen unless we really want to see them," said their mother, who had started to clean the area in preparation for construction.

"What are these ladies talking about? What about us extra-terrestrial forces, who are here to help you achieve your dreams?" Ms Destiny did not like that her existence was not accepted; however, before she left, Magical Love came with the new magic potion.

"Hmm, you seem low-spirited," said Magical Love. But without waiting for an answer, he said, "This is another brew, but it is the last potion of the year. I have no more ingredients left and would have to source them after this mission is over.'

"So, how do we get her to drink it?" asked Magical Love.

"It is not as easy as last night. Look at all of them. Who knows who is going to drink what, when, or where?"

"I cannot predict it. The future-teller might, and he will be here soon."

"I might try something; are you ready to shake things up?"

"Oh god, I totally forgot that part. No, you cannot do it now. The women already suspect something is in the backyard," said Ms Destiny.

"Well, they can suspect as much as they like. They cannot see us, though. We are well-hidden under the cloak."

"I know; however, if they think that there is a thief in the backyard, then more people will be called in, which would only make things difficult for us."

"I agree there," said Magical Love.

"Thanks. Now we have to wait for them to make tea and then find an opportunity to dissolve the potion in Phloxia's drink."

"I like your idea. It is better, though, that it is done before the psychic shows up, for the moment he puts his foot in, he is going to start working out a plan for Phloxia, for he will be completely under the influence of my magic potion by now, and if Phloxia does not have the magic potion, it will not make any sense to her."

"Oh, all this is so confusing. Hopefully, your magic potion has worked for the future-teller," said Ms Destiny.

"What do you mean by your hope? It certainly has, for, yes, I might make a mistake once, but twice? That has never happened before. I am a living example of only making a mistake once. Don't worry, you woman in the cloak with a throbbing heart. It will all work out for us. If I have decided that you will win, then I will make sure that you do." Magical Love knew what he was saying, for three c's: confidence, creativity and conquest always followed him everywhere.

Finally, the opportunity came to add the magic potion to Phloxia's drink when Abelia asked Paulia to make some tea, for she needed a kick of energy to keep working through the night.

"Why don't you have some rest?" Phloxia asked her mother.

"Oh, Phloxia, I will rest when the kitchen is ready."

"But, Mother, it will take months," said Phloxia.

"Then we will take turns; either you will be working or I will be. Do some cleaning of the bricks while I am having tea,' said her mother, washing her hands.

"No, I am not doing that," said Phloxia, shaking her head and looking at her sisters.

"It will not take long for Mother to drink tea, Phloxia. Wash some bricks. I will pass your tea there," said Villiea.

Phloxia did not want to go, but then she felt sympathy for her mother, who had been working all day long, so she went to do the washing of bricks anyway.

Paulia and Villiea looked at each other and smiled to see Phloxia washing bricks when she would never wash dishes when asked by them.

That was the perfect moment for Magical Love to mix his magic potion into Phloxia's tea. At the same time, Ms Destiny shook the tree. Paulia and Villiea, however, did not take much notice of the shaking tree, for it was daylight.

"I hope she drinks it," said Ms Destiny.

Phloxia did drink the tea without any major issues except that she might have added in some water from washing the bricks.

Then came the man for whom everyone had been waiting for a long, long time; Augur the Psychic entered the house with Yarrow Dron.

Paulia went to get tea from the kitchen, for she always made sure to have extra tea as a sign of generosity.

The crystal gazer and Yarrow Dron got comfortable in their chairs. Paulia gave them tea.

"Hmm, there is something unquestionably out there in the backyard," said Augur the Psychic, looking towards the tree, where Ms Destiny and Magical Love were standing under the invisible cape.

"Why is everyone pointing at us?" said Ms Destiny. "Are you sure they cannot see us?"

"I am pretty sure that Augur cannot see us, for he is on my drug, and the only thing he is to see is the way to the land of Wellingtonia for Phloxia. However, my only worry is that Phloxia just had the magic potion, so it might need an hour or two before it kicks in. If somehow this crystal gazer could do the reading tomorrow, that would make my plan faultless."

And the wish of Magical Love came true when Yarrow looked at the yard and said the same thing. "Hmm, I have a hunch, too, that there might be something in the yard. Something that we cannot see."

"It could be your brother," said Abelia, who was back at work. "He was the one who planted the tree and had an intense liking for it. He loved to be around it and sit under it."

"What happened to her?" asked Augur the Psychic, looking at Abelia working on the new kitchen and seeming more competent than a builder.

"Don't know; there was some shaking of the tree around midnight, and since then, Abelia has been shaken and acting weird."

"Hmm," said Augur. "So I am here to help her? I can see she is under the influence of some extra-terrestrial object."

"No," said Yarrow Dron. "We want you to help Phloxia, for she sometimes acts all right, and other days, goes completely wild and doesn't listen or says things that do not make any sense."

"Hmm." Augur the Psychic looked at Phloxia, who had finished her tea and was looking in the void and to the third person; she was staring at the tree.

"It seems this tree is an issue. I will sleep under this tree tonight, and because I am sleeping under the tree, no one else will be able to, and anything that we cannot see will have to leave.

Also, it is good to start my treatment in the morning so we can all see the end result in daylight, for the end result can be too dark to be seen in the dark."

"Hmm," agreed Yarrow Dron. "I will sleep here tonight too. Abelia, what do you think?" asked Yarrow.

"Right. You two can help me renovate the kitchen before bed. It is still a couple of hours before the sun sets," said Abelia.

"You have to believe me. She needs help too," said Augur the Psychic, looking at Yarrow Dron.

Both Villiea and Paulia were looking at Phloxia, who, by now, was not blinking at all and was acting as if she could see something out in the backyard.

"There is undoubtedly something in the backyard, Villiea," said Paulia.

"I should not have talked about ghosts earlier," said Villiea to Paulia.

They both went to Phloxia to ask for her help with cooking dinner. "What are you looking at Phloxia?" asked Paulia hesitantly.

"I am trying to look for my lost soul," said Phloxia.

"I take my theory back about Rocko the Thief. It is a ghost or spirit or, indeed, something extra-terrestrial," said Paulia, looking at both Phloxia and Abelia.

"Let's finish cooking the dinner, so tomorrow in daylight, hopefully, the crystal gazer will show us the end result and get everything back to normal." Both sisters started cooking, for it was futile to ask Phloxia anymore, and there was no point asking their mother either.

"What about us?" Ms Destiny asked Magical Love.

"Hmm, I am hungry too, and we might have to leave for the night anyway, for Augur the Psychic is sleeping under the tree."

"Hmm, are you sure he is on your magic potion, though?" again asked Ms Destiny.

"Oh, indeed, he is. Without the magic potion, he would not dare to sleep under this famous tree."

"Okay, I believe you. Let's go for dinner too." Both Ms Destiny and Magical Love left.

"Everything will be in order tomorrow. Phloxia will accept her dormant feelings for Deutzo Hydrang. Augur will show her the path. The God of Humanity will give her the courage to walk on that path, and both love and destiny will win."

"Sounds like a good plan, unless something happens," said Ms Destiny.

"Why are you so negative? Do you eat electrons for dessert?" said Magical Love, smiling and assuring her everything would be all right.

They had dinner, again with Magical Love being a proton, and Ms Destiny, an electron.

On the way back home, they met the feral cats going back to the abandoned container.

They overheard them talking. "Oh no, she is going crazy, for she just became a mum," said one of the cats, who was wearing bright red heels and a floral skirt with her tail slightly visible from behind.

"Oh no, she is going crazy, for she is high on milk from this morning," said one of the other cats, who was wearing a suit, as she had just finished the work of chasing the rats all day long.

"Whatever the reason, however, Tabby the Cat has announced that she will never go to work again because she is trying to think of something for someone. The strange part is that she does not know anyone named 'someone'," said the cat with the high heels and floral skirt.

"What were they talking about?" said Ms Destiny.

"I would not know, and who cares about feral cats?" said Magical Love.

"I am domesticated," said the one with the suit, giving an angry look to Magical Love.

"Better stay invisible," said Magical Love, hiding again.

"Yes, the world is quite unpredictable these days," repeated Magical Love.

"Well, you could have guessed. Domesticated is sophisticated!" remarked Ms Destiny.

"That means ferals wear floral." Both Magical Love and Ms Destiny could not stop laughing, for Ms Destiny was also wearing a floral dress.

They went to Ms Destiny's place to sleep.

"We might go to see the D. Drons very early tomorrow morning," said Ms Destiny.

"Sure, wake me up at midnight."

"Midnight?" asked Ms Destiny.

"I want to make sure that Phloxia has gone feral by then and is not acting domesticated, for the sake of my plan and her happy life."

They both slept, and so did everyone at the D. Dron residence.

Before long, Ms Destiny nudged Magical Love to wake him up. He was making roaring sounds like the crow that Cyclamen D. Manhood owned.

"Something bad is going to happen," said Ms Destiny as soon as Magical Love was up. "You were snoring like Cyclamen D. Manhood's godfather."

"Stop acting like Abelia. I want some coffee before we

leave."

"Make one for me too," said Ms Destiny, getting comfortable in her favourite chair.

"Sure."

Magical Love and Ms Destiny had invisible coffee in their invisible cups, and after finishing the coffee, they went straight to the D. Dron residence.

Phloxia was sleeping and dreaming for now. She found herself in the land of Wellingtonia, a beautiful land, filled with flowers of all colours and mainly conifer trees, for it had plenty of rainfall, cool winters, and warm summers. *The trees might be different, but the weather is the same as my land,* thought Phloxia in her dream.

Then she saw a dark forest and her man. His face was very clear this time, and nothing mattered to her except him. 'Are you real?' she asked.

"As real as your feelings," he replied.

"He is real," said Phloxia in her dream and woke up, and from then on, neither did she sleep nor let anyone else sleep.

Thus, when Magical Love and Ms Destiny arrived, this completely different situation was unfolding.

Phloxia was drawing something in her notebook. Abelia, who had been woken up by all these noises, had started working on her kitchen in the middle of the night.

Both of Phloxia's sisters were looking at her to predict if she would renovate the bedroom or the bathroom, for their mother took responsibility for the kitchen.

Yarrow Dron was trying to wake up Augur the Psychic, who had no idea what was happening and was still asleep.

Ms Destiny looked at Magical Love. "The plan is

operational, Ms Destiny. Phloxia now believes in what she saw and is trying to figure out how to get there by plotting graphs and drawing maps to predict her success. You will see that Augur the Psychic will sense her role and help her by showing her the right path."

"I hope so," said Ms Destiny.

Augur the Psychic was puzzled as soon as he woke up. He looked around, and everything seemed very unusual to him. A regular midnight ritual usually involved sleeping, especially in the land of Aliesalba, where 'early to bed and early to rise' was the motto for a successful, natural life that flows freely like a river and otherwise is stagnant like a leaf in the mud.

"It would be best if you did something," said Yarrow Dron. "For Phloxia is acting like her mother. She seems to be on something, but her glass of water is still there, so it must be something else."

"Oh, Yarrow. It is a very unusual scene for me. I have not come across such a situation where I've had to use my exceptional skills in the middle of the night. If I start my treatment now, it will be too dark for you to see the end result."

"That is all right as long as you can see it," said Yarrow Dron.

"Hmm, I will need a cup of tea, though. I cannot work without having a cup of tea," said Augur the Psychic.

"I can arrange that," said Yarrow, and he asked Paulia to make tea.

Augur the Psychic looked at Phloxia and her drawings. "What are you drawing, my dear child?" he asked.

"Ways to make dreams a reality," said Phloxia.

"Does not sound that bad to me," said Augur the Psychic, grabbing the cup of tea.

Everyone, including Ms Destiny and Magical Love, were

looking at Augur the Psychic to see if he could come up with a plan to help Phloxia find what her heart was seeking.

Instead, that spectacular moment came sooner rather than later, when Augur the Psychic said, after finishing his tea, "The tea was superb. Early morning tea is my weakness, and I do not wake up until I have one. Now I understand why I was not absorbing all that is happening here. I will tell you what happened yesterday. While I was asleep, something stole my milk—not sure if it was pregnant cats or mad dogs—that I need for making tea in the morning. So, I did not have tea in the morning, and I have been out of my mind until now." After that, he continued talking.

Ms Destiny and Magical Love could not listen anymore, for Ms Destiny was questioning Magical Love and his three c's and was cursing her fate for trusting him.

Back at Ms Destiny's house, the two gods tried to decide what to do.

"What now?" asked Ms Destiny, looking at Magical Love.

"What that group of domesticated and feral cats were talking about makes sense now. Tabby the Cat must have stolen milk from Augur the Psychic."

"I have to do this now. I was trying to avoid it, but not anymore. I will go and visit the D. Drons in the morning," said Ms Martini.

"No, you cannot do this," said Magical Love. "What about the rules?"

"Rules are not important when it comes to saving a life. What looks like an amusing situation will now end up as a tragedy. We took lives from two lovebirds and created human lives, making it challenging for the soulmates to find each other. However, it is not about love yet."

"Here, I see one lovebird struggling to find her identity and confused to a point where dreams have taken over reality, and reality has its claws on the dreams. I might be breaking the rules, but these rules were made after creating the situation, when everyone started to think about their own benefit, their own wins. No one cares about how poor Phloxia is suffering."

"Also, it is not only about Phloxia. It is about my rules. It is about the rules that govern the purpose of my existence. Whenever an individual struggles and makes an effort to change their fate, I shall be there, and that is what I am doing. I am going to rule the bloody rules because I don't allow rules to rule me. Also, next time you make a love potion, make sure to guard it overnight. Now, go and help that tabby cat."

Ms Destiny waited for sunrise to go and see the D. Drons, and with the first ray of sun, she knocked on the door.

Paulia opened the door and was surprised to see Ms Martini there.

This time, Villiea went to make tea. Phloxia and everyone else looked at Ms Martini as soon as she entered the house.

Abelia did not pay much attention, for she was busy doing the kitchen.

Paulia introduced Ms Martini to Yarrow, for he was meeting her for the first time.

"We might talk to you some other day, Ms Martini, for we have a difficult situation here today," said Yarrow Dron to Ms Martini.

"I heard about it," said Ms Martini and looked around. "I came here to help."

"How could you help?" said Yarrow Dron. "There is no way we are sending Phloxia away again. It is lousy timing. Phloxia will be getting married very soon. There is a family, and the man is well-settled. So we do not need any help here. Sorry, Ms Martini," said Yarrow Dron as if in a rush for Ms Destiny to leave.

"Oh, you found someone for Phloxia. Next time, make sure to ask me, for matchmaking is my second business. It is a kind of hobby," said Augur the Psychic.

"Find me one," said Yarrow. He felt like everyone around him was talking about things unrelated to the issue at hand.

"A woman for you? About what age?" asked Augur the Psychic.

Yarrow gave him a look as if he couldn't believe what he was hearing.

"So, Ms Martini, please excuse us today, for we have people here who are waiting for outsiders to leave."

"I know, Yarrow Dron, but I also have some ability in fortune-telling." Ms Martini got the multi-skilling idea from Augur the Psychic.

"We already have a psychic here," said Yarrow, "and I suggest everyone concentrate on their primary business."

"What happened to Abelia?" Ms Martini tried to change the topic.

"You better go, Ms Martini, and do not show up unless someone from my family calls you here. Whatever we have here will be sorted." With that, Yarrow pointed her to the door.

"Can I please talk to Phloxia for two minutes?" Ms Martini asked Yarrow.

Yarrow realised that Ms Martini would not leave otherwise, so he unwillingly allowed that to happen.

Ms Martini knew she only had two minutes, so she hid a letter in a book and gave it to Phloxia. She told Phloxia it was a good read, and then she left.

"Come here," instructed Yarrow, and Phloxia put the book aside and went to Yarrow.

"You, Augur the Psychic. Do you know the business you are here for? If you do, then do your job and leave, for I have had enough. This is my brother's family, not a playground for anyone to come anytime and do anything, whenever they like."

"Oh, sure," said Augur the Psychic. He started looking at Phloxia and asked her to show him her hand. "She has come here without finishing her journey in her last birth, so her soul is seeking the past that does not exist in this life," said Augur.

"It does not matter what the problem is, Augur. Tell us the solution," demanded Yarrow, who wanted to stay on point and only focus on things that he could do something about and not waste time on anything else.

"That is difficult to think of," said Augur the Psychic.
"All right, then. Come back when you have one," said Yarrow Dron, showing him the door.
"Oh, no, Yarrow. You are a little highly strung today. I mean, it will be difficult for only two minutes. Make another tea, and I will think of something."

Yarrow Dron asked Paulia to make tea and said it would be the last one for the day.

"See, there are a couple of reasons why issues from past births are transferred. One reason is that something could not be attained in the last birth; thus, life gives the participant another life to achieve the end result. Another reason is that someone, like a superpower, takes the participant's life and uses it to play a game."

"It does not matter to me what or why, Augur the Psychic. You have one minute to think up a solution."

"Dear Phloxia is doomed to have a life that will only end in tragedy. It does not matter what she or you decide to do. Her fate cannot be changed," said Augur the Psychic. It was unclear whether he said that because he was angry about the way Yarrow Dron was talking to him or because it was the truth.

"All right. I will take it from here," said Yarrow and showed him the way out.

"Girls, we have seen what is going on around here. Phloxia is doomed, either way, as that idiot said. Your mother has developed skills that would otherwise require special knowledge. I want to request that you both stay here and not allow anyone in, and do not go out until tomorrow."

I will visit the family whose son is interested in marrying Phloxia for whatever reasons. Try to help your mother so the kitchen is done, and she can have some rest.

"I will come back soon. Don't worry; there is nothing under that tree, and if it is Rhondo D. Dron's ghost, then it's still all right, for he was your father."

"Yes, Uncle," said all the girls, including Phloxia, who had a desire awoken in her now because of the magic potion. Still, she was trying to come up with sensible ways of achieving what she wanted, and was not lost anymore. She had a set aim to meet the man of her dreams, like her mother had a set purpose of renovating the kitchen, and she was working on it, tirelessly and with focus, without allowing anything or anyone to get in her way because she could see the path, and Phloxia was yet to see her way.

The girls sat on chairs. Paulia and Villiea were smiling at each other, for the D. Drons were famous for nonsense genes, and now they would be famous for nonsense sightings too.

"All that matters is to be famous," said Paulia.

"Oh, yes, like your husband's family is famous for their

family name, D. Homo Sapien." And they both laughed while their mother was renovating the kitchen.

Phloxia said she would have a short nap, for they had been up since midnight, and the other two girls also decided to sleep for a bit. They suggested their mother should take a break too, but she declined and said she would rest when finished, for a desire is only a want unless it is burning.

Paulia and Villiea just shrugged their shoulders and went to sleep.

Phloxia looked at her and thought about how quickly something can change if you really want it to change, and how quickly anything can be attained if the true desire is there, or if there was, as her mother had put it, 'a burning desire'.

She then decided to read the book that Ms Martini had left with her, *Hidden Desires to Destiny*. The book read:

A desire, a wish, a want, and a hope all come from within you. They are yours. You own them. You see them. You live in them, and they live in you. They are as alive as you are, yet you are hesitant to accept their presence, and while doing so, you are denying your own being. It takes a heart to make a move, for we have thousands of fears. The irony is, though, we decide to live with fears all our lives rather than express ourselves. By suppressing ourselves, we express the one who is accepted in society. Still, if that makes you happy, by all means, do that, but if it doesn't, then think for a minute, and shake things up, even the tree in your backyard.

"Really?" said Phloxia to herself, looking at the tree in her own backyard. "Maybe people who do not have a tree in their backyard have been coming here to shake ours; that explains the shaking last night and this afternoon, right?" And she started looking at the whole book and found a note in it.

Phloxia,

I know you have a desire that wants to meet its destiny. I know you are seeking a path but do not have anyone to show you the right path. I want to help you, for I know that it takes a lot to follow one's desires to get to destiny. That is the only difference between fate and destiny.

Fate, you live, and destiny lives in you and makes you alive. Desire is the seedling, and it comes from your heart. Unless you believe in it, the seed will not become a seedling and, eventually, a fully-fledged tree with the fruit of your desires, leaves of your happiness and the shade of satisfaction, and all that would reflect in your face, in your eyes. It can all happen with the first step of believing in your desires, and I know you believe in them, for you know that the reason for your unhappiness is that any happiness does not touch your heart. Your heart is somewhere else. Your heart is already there, where it is trying to take you by showing you the path by asking you to accept the visions and make a move.

I am here for you. The next ship will be leaving in two weeks. I know your family would never agree, but do you agree? If you do, then come to my address in two weeks, and if not, then please read the book, for at least you will know the reason for your unhappiness and will be able to learn to live with it.

Ms Martini
131 The Ocean View
Waves Island
The Land of Aliesalba

Phloxia read the note again and thought, *How is it possible that I could leave without telling anyone? Even though I like what is in my dreams, and I do want it, still, it does not change the fact that I am on the other side of the world in a family with their own ways of life. And even if I do go there, who can guarantee that I will meet this man, or that this man will be seeking my arrival, or that the love story will have a happy ending? If love was that easy to attain, then it would not be so prohibited in society, and the one where I live has extra restrictions on it, as with the word 'hidden' even though it is very prevalent in our home.*

Look at my mum, such a dedication she shows for work. My sisters are sleeping soundly. My uncle comes here only because he is worried about me. They all want me to get to my destiny or fate, whatever is prevalent here, and see my wedding day. They are trying so hard, so would it be wrong if I let them get what they want? Would it be wrong If I live the way they want me to live?

Oh, that sounds a little wrong; let's change the question. Would it be wrong to stay happy forever to make others happy?

No, it would not be, and it is not. I am going to do what others want me to do, for that is the way that runs in our blood, and that blood has been running in our arteries, and veins and capillaries for generations. Generations and generations have lived this way, so who am I to complain? Or question? A woman with no life experience, with her own thoughts and big dreams? That does not make me special. I am one of them. And as Villiea said, reality does not change. Rather you change your dreams to match with reality. That is the way to have a happy life.

I am going to change my dreams and will dream about what I am allowed to dream.

She threw that letter in the rubbish bin, which was collected every other day, and today was that other day, so, unfortunately, that letter lay on the bottom of the bin in the same way that Phloxia's desire now resided in the bottom of her heart and let forced dreams step on it, and new rubbish piled on her last hope of meeting her true love.

On another side of the world, Ms Destiny and Magical Love were again having invisible coffee in invisible cups.

"Let us go and see The God of Humanity," said Ms Destiny to Magical Love.

"Oh, I have not made the appointment yet," said Magical Love.

"We will be all right," said Ms Destiny. "Let's go."

"What do you have to talk about?"

"Unfairness," said Ms Destiny.

"As you say, you are the ruler," said Magical Love, and they both went to where The God of Humanity lived, in a small but beautiful house away from the city on a small farm. As they got there, he was watering the flowers on his farm.

"Sorry, God. We did not make an appointment," said Magical Love.

"You must have really wanted to see me, so you found me," said The God of Humanity as he motioned for them to sit on the soil next to the flowers. "Feel the earth and the grass. May they tenderise your soul and fulfil your desires."

"The God of Humanity, this is not fair. Phloxia has no help, and we took life from lovebirds, so we owe them something."

"Dear Destiny, we have not taken their lives. We gave them new lives, whole new lives to love and spread love," said The God of Humanity.

"But, The God of Humanity, why does she have to put in all the effort? What about Deutzo Hydrang? Can't we make him come to her? Is it not unfair that she is suffering while Deutzo is enjoying his royal status?"

"You know the answer, Destiny; you do. Phloxia, even if Deutzo came to her, would not be able to accept him, for she would not be able to believe that a royal had come to their home just like that. The excitement would give her the feeling of his generosity but not love. To feel love for him and for him to feel love towards her, she needs to earn it, and if you ask why Phloxia could not be born as a royal, then you know the answer; what a woman can do, a man cannot. You and Phloxia are the women in this situation. I am proud of you both. Having said that, men do have their role in society. I admire them too," said The God of Humanity, looking at Magical Love. "However, a lion is born to a lioness, and a lion is not as strong as a lioness."

"I don't get it," said Magical Love.

"Any mother can become a lioness when the situation calls for it. Think what a lioness can become when circumstances demand it. A man is always a man, as a lion is always a lion. That is the difference, and that difference matters when it comes to achieving love. Are you satisfied, Ms Destiny?" asked The God of Humanity.

"I am, The God of Humanity."

"Do you have any questions, Magical Love?" asked The God of Humanity, looking at Magical Love.

"One question, The God of Humanity. Who is going to win this challenge?"

"Whoever has the most desire to win. Anyhow, it is time for me to talk to my creations," said The God of Humanity, signalling towards his farm of flowers, and, thus, Magical Love and Ms Destiny left.

"The God of Humanity is very kind," said Magical Love.
"Hmm, what about me?" said Ms Destiny.
"You are my woman. I have to say you are kind," said Magical

Love, smiling.

"Oh, yea, I remember now rather something else; what is going on in Wellingtonia now? What is Mad Solo up to? I mean, we are worried about Phloxia but if Prince Deutzo Hydrang has to leave straight after marriage, then lovebirds never be together. I can't believe that I believed you on this by recruiting Mad Solo, who changed the whole course of life on Wellingtonia" asked Ms Destiny in curiosity.

"Wow, thanks for reminding me; I totally forgot to get updates on that and hope the lioness of Wellingtonia the Queen Mother has gone back to the normal genome, so you won't keep blaming me forever," said Magical Love.

"Yea go and get updates, and I rather want to sleep for a while," said Ms Destiny.

So, Magical Love started checking the situation in Wellingtonia while Ms Destiny slept.

Wellingtonia was going through a situation no one could make any sense of, for Queen Mother had become something more than a lioness who was of a danger to the race of men, partially due to her bad experience with her husband. However, a ray of hope arrived with the arrival of Mad Solo, who promised that he would convince Queen Mother to let him hover around her, for a couple of days, by praising her dominance and the decision to throw men out of their homes wearing one earring. Using this strategy, he planned to observe her genome and rectify it.

The scientist Mad Solo thus planted himself around the dominant genome. At first sight, he was blown away by the inducement power of Queen Mother's genetic mutation, caused by an escapee spider, and her anger towards men to her abandonment by her king husband. Mad Solo's fuses were blown by seeing this extraordinary event; that led to an occurrence of another remarkable event, for as he felt 'The Force' of Queen Mother's all dominant genes, his eyes popped out. From that day onwards, he had to be kept in forced quarantine for two weeks before letting him loose in the streets of Wellingtonia. As he had become a danger to the entire population with his eyes popped out, after looking at such a rare genome, and had threatening behaviour toward everyone in her vicinity.

After quarantine, he went to see the men around the lake with his eyes permanently popped. Mad Solo told all the men the dangers of dominant genome for oncoming generations as indescribable. We need a superpower to help us, was the solution he suggested.

"But how and where would we get a superpower?" Asked Prince Deutzo, who kept visiting the men living around the abandoned lake, as moral support to them and him.

"I felt immense force, call it 'The Force' around the Queen Mother, and someone needs to take 'The Force' away; Only a superpower could have the calibre to remove the force from around the Queen Mother." Mad Solo described his findings.

"A Superpower?" asked Prince Deutzo Hydrang.

"Hmm, very powerful one that knows all about the force of an all dominant genome. There are two steps now to get rid of the killer genome of Queen Mother."

"I will build a nuclear reactor that would produce the superpower, the next part might shock you, so please take a shock absorbent seat," said Mad Solo moving around, "Once the superpower is formed, a man with faulty genome will take it to Spiderman's genome to remove the force. Once the force is removed from around the killer genome; faulty genome can access the deadly genome and take away its deadliness," explained Mad Solo. Hearing this, everyone went into 220 voltage shock; however, due to shock-absorbent seating, no damage was reported.

"I understand," said Prince Deutzo, "that Superpower would come out of the reactor; however, where would the faulty genome come out from?'

"Dear Prince Deutzo Hydrang, I know a place filled with faulty genome; I only need to figure out who out of all is suitable for our task and how would it get here. I am still shocked from seeing your mother's genome, but give me some time and let me build the nuclear reactor. Once the device to produce the superpower is finalised, I will figure a way out to get the work done from the faulty genome."

"Hmm", said Prince Deutzo Hydrang, and all other men were happy, for at least there was hope now for their freedom from the killer genome and all other equally dominant women of Wellingtonia.

Prince Deutzo went back to the palace and was in complete shock when Queen Mother gave him a piece of fresh news, fresh as the morning sun.

Queen Mother told Prince Deutzo that because she has all dominant genome, thus she wants to find a woman of her calibre for him to rule Wellingtonia after her. However, because she is not a scientist, the only way to test the potency of a genome is through a unique device whose design she got from the books of history. The device, named 'Nail the fish's eye', is a potent instrument to recognise the wild genome type. She tested her genome on it, and only she could successfully pass the test offered by this device, out of all other women and men who took part in her experiment.

"So for you, Prince Deutzo, she continued, I have arranged

'The most eligible bachelor of Wellingtonia'. Princesses from all over the world will be invited to Wellingtonia to compete and establish the dominancy of their genome. Whoever could shoot the fish's eye using a bow and an arrow will be rendered a winner and the right candidate to marry you, evict you in the wild to join the other men lots."

Mother, I was not expecting that from you, said Prince Deutzo Hydrang, almost crying.

"What were you expecting from me then, Prince Deutzo? Perhaps you should remember that I wear clothes with dominant written on them for a reason. I am an all dominant genome," said Queen Mother.

"I wanted you to be my mother. I wanted a woman who would have gentle feelings. You arranged 'The whatever bachelor' for me without telling me and this instrument of yours to test the potency of a genome? I mean, do you even know what you do, mother? You sound and act like a superman. Still, all I am getting is a ruthless Superman dancing around me all day." Prince Deutzo was sending distress signals to save him, but unfortunately, no one was around to read his distress.

"You are lucky dear that Superman is dancing", said Queen Mother dancing. "For if it was not dancing, you would already be evicted without any piercing to join the lot that you go and check on every other day, said Queen Mother jumping up and down the roof and left.

Prince Deutzo Hydrang could not sleep and wished for a woman to show him what a tender woman looks like. He knew that all the women in Wellingtonia are dominant thus dreamt of a woman from another land to whom he could open up about his fear of women lot. Then, as if his wish came true, he found himself with a woman in a dark, dark forest far away from civilisation, and he started the conversation.

"I am simply scared of women, all women of Wellingtonia. I am only talking to you, for you are from another land. If I must tell you, the women here are so deadly that they cannot stand a man's touch. They hate us. I mean, what have we done to earn so much hate?"

"Did you come here because you are scared of women? Open up to me, Prince Deutzo, don't worry; I have got you covered from all sorts of genomes, deadly or not. Tell me, tell me more. I want to hear you do all the talking, all night without any fears," said the woman from another land with Deutzo's head on her shoulder.

"I am not sure if you would want to hear it, or it might scare you, or you might feel that how could a prince be so weak?"

"Don't worry about that anymore, Prince Deutzo, for I already know your weakness; once you are done with your fears, I have a few too to enlighten you and might make you feel better," the woman in his dreams said.

Prince Deutzo pulled her hair away from her face. He lay down on the ground with his head placed in a woman from another land's lap, who was now sitting with her back touching the big stem of a big tree as Prince Deutzo got ready to tell Phloxia his life story, the sky full of stars turned into dark clouds filled with water. It started to drizzle as if clouds were helping Prince Deutzo open up, for telling about one's hidden world becomes more straightforward in the dark, and drizzle was helping to hide the tearing emotions of Prince Deutzo. It takes a lot for a man to disclose his hidden world, and God must know it.

"I lived in the palace my whole life. I had everything and

could get anything. However, being surrounded by only women, who act in a certain way, talk in a certain way; made me feel detached from everything, for I could not do that and felt as if something was wrong with me."

"Then, fortunately, I found this place, and I came here the first time by accident for it was raining so hard to see anything; my horse lost its way and got me here. First, I thought of it as a dark, scary forest filled with daunting noises and wild animals; then, I had to stay here for a while, for I had no way to go back in the rain and storm. As I sat there, I realised that I was not in this place, but this place was in me. I felt as if this place was in me forever, and finally, it had come out and become this forest."

"The darkness was my darkness, the one that is inside me, the daunting noises was my inner voice that wanted to yell, cry and tell the whole world that I want to be free of Spiderman's genome torture, and those wild animals were me, who could do what they want, go where they wanted. The rain and storm were all me. This place was not a forest from then on. It was the place I became myself; from there on, every time I felt sad, I would escape in the middle of the night and spend my time here looking at the sky and talking to the stars, everything I wished. All I wanted then was you, even though I did not know you."

"I wanted to marry someone from the world that was away from my world; An independent woman with an average genome, but now Spiderman's genome has a perfect plan to find all dominant genomes for me. If I married a deadly genome, it never could see me, for they only see perfect genome, and I live with a genome full of recessive genes."

"I only wish it might become possible for me to spend my life with you, but for that, you have to prove that you are dominant and you are not. How would you win?"

"Deutzo, I am feeling the gravitas of the dominant genome now before I thought it was funny. Don't worry, my love, I am here and will always stand with you, will never pierce your ear and will never let you lose in the wild. I will fight for your rights; even better, I will fight for the freedom of men of Wellingtonia and make sure to get men equal rights as women, except the childbearing capacity," assured the woman in the dream.

It was drizzling, and the prince's face was covered with the raindrops that made it hard to see the tears; however, Prince Deutzo had shown his heart to a woman from another land, so how could he hide his tears from her?

As a tear touched his cheek, Prince Deutzo realised he was sleeping on his chair on the balcony, and rain had covered his face in water. Prince Deutzo moved into his room and wished for a woman with the average genome in his life to come true. It hopefully would change Wellingtonia's men's plight in the hands of women with full-on dominance genome, with not one-two but all forty-six dominant genes. So much dominance never seen before and never will be, for it only happens in Wellingtonia.

Magical love was back by morning to have coffee with Ms Destiny and gave her the updates. After hearing all these, Ms Destiny said, "Hmm, 'the most eligible bachelor of Wellingtonia', interesting. That could help. but, let's go then and see the D. Drons and check what is going on, for today, a man and his family are coming to arrange the wedding date. I also want to see if Phloxia has read my letter yet or not."

"I want to see how the renovations are tracking," Magical Love said and laughed again.

As they talked, they got to the D. Dron residence, where everyone was getting ready. Abelia was still in the kitchen, and it was almost done anyway, for she had not slept since starting the project.

"How are you feeling, Phloxia?" asked Paulia.

"I am feeling great," said Phloxia.

"Phloxia, dear, one has to live life, and that is the rule. We want to see you happy, and we know that accepting what you have is the way to a happy life," said Villiea.

"I know, Villiea, and I am ready to start a new chapter in my life by forgetting anything that is not part of reality."

That was a relief for the whole family, except for Abelia, who was still in the kitchen and was not listening to any of it.

Then there came the big event that everyone had been waiting for since the birth of Phloxia D. Dron. This was the first time the family was seeing the man who was to marry Phloxia. And the second time would be on the day of the wedding. He looked like a normal Aliesalbian. He had two eyes, one nose, two ears and a fair amount of hair, and he did represent an average citizen.

They all sat while Paulia went to make tea. Yarrow was head of the house today, for Abelia was busy doing her work.

"This is our beautiful Phloxia. She is smart and good at reading, for she has been to the Institute of Theoretical Knowledge of Social Skills."

"Our boy is the best too. We used to live close to feral cats, and he started working, and now we live on the high street," said the man's mother.

"What is Phloxia's mother doing?" asked the lady.

"She is getting the kitchen ready for Phloxia. She always wished to have a new kitchen for her wedding day, and, thus, her mother is making sure to finish it as soon as possible—as a matter of urgency, in fact, for we want the wedding to be sooner rather than later. Phloxia's sisters are married and, thus, it is time that

Phloxia also found her way to another house."

'That is what we want too,' said the lady. 'I would get someone's help with the chores, like cleaning the clothes and washing the dishes, for that is the most important work. That is the work that we ladies cannot get enough of. Still, I would not mind giving some to Phloxia."

"We D. Drons are famous for our daughters knowing all this by heart. Phloxia has theoretical knowledge anyway, and you can show her the practical skills of every day, and I am sure that she will learn eventually, if not very soon." Yarrow was trying to be honest so as not to have any issues in the future.

They all finished tea, and then the man and his family left, with an agreement that the wedding would be in five days. It would be a simple wedding that would suit both families.

Yarrow asked Abelia if she would be all right with that. Abelia looked at the kitchen and said, "Yes, this will be done by then, so you can lock it in."

Yarrow then sat with the girls and asked them to make the preparations and call in other family members, and he left to make more arrangements himself, like buying things and so on.

"I do not think Phloxia will be doing as I asked her to do," said Ms Destiny to Magical Love, who was sitting on the portable bed, under the tree that was still there from the night Augur the Psychic had slept on it.

"I know, and there is nothing we can do anymore. We tried, and it seems that her fate is too strong to be beaten by her destiny. At the end of the day, she has to do things for herself. She has to realise the power of her destiny and use it. We can help her, show her the right path, and clear the track for her. However, she needs to walk on it herself. You are the destiny, and Phloxia must do something others have not done to claim it."

"That was the purpose of separating the lovebirds and giving them so many challenges—to prove that anyone can do anything. If you gift her everything on a golden plate, it will only debunk The God of Humanity's words, which neither of us wants. Also, Wellingtonia's future is in jeopardy anyways, and not sure how Phloxia would fit in there, unless her defective genome does wonders."

"We have tried enough, Ms Destiny, and more than enough. Instead, I would say, it is time to leave her to her own devices and let her figure out her own life. If nothing happens, and the lovebirds never meet, then The God of Humanity will take his claim of equality and fairness back. At least the illusion of good will be gone. You will be going back to heaven and leaving the earth, for you know that no matter how much you try, fate rules. I will never be satisfied because I need two hearts to feel fulfilled, but this world seems too practical to allow anything that does not fit its criteria. People are too scared to follow their hearts and do what they want; their brains are filled with the mythological content of only one way, to walk in a straight line with blindfolded eyes. They are happy to see what others see, and they make it their truth and feel proud of it." Magical Love was quite emotional.

"Excellent speech," said Ms Destiny. "I did not know you were so sentimental. but what about the mess in Wellingtonia that you and your friend The Mad Solo created?"

"Oh, forgot about that, the explanation is that I only sent in the Mad Solo, however, that poor spider whose daylight was knocked out had gone there on Mr Fate's orders. So I am sure something would happen itself as I do not want to involve Mad

Solo here in Aliesalba for I can't predict the consequence of his actions from now on," said Magical Love, and they both departed, as Ms Destiny looked at him in disbelief and prayed to the God Of Humanity for Wellingtonia and left Phloxia on her own to realise or not realise that she needed to reclaim the love that was taken from her.

Phloxia started helping her mother, and soon, the kitchen was as her mother desired, or at least good enough to satisfy her.

Her mother finally sat, and Paulia gave her the tea.

Abelia took a long breath, looked at the kitchen, and said that she had never had such a feeling before, a feeling of satisfaction and immense pleasure, not because her dream of having an improved kitchen was fulfilled, but because she had worked to get it; she earned it.

"The sense of achieving your desire makes your whole being content. It makes you realise what you are capable of when you throw yourself into the well of your dreams only to come out when they are fulfilled; this feeling cannot come in any other way."

Phloxia looked at her mum and wondered whether her mother had matched her dreams with reality or changed the reality to achieve her dreams.

"Mother, that was an easy dream; you could have done it years ago," said Villiea.

"I could have. I think I could have if I'd wanted it as badly as I do now. It seems someone did not shake our tree that night but shook me. Anyhow, we have a wedding in a couple of days, so we better get ready," said Abelia, putting her cup of tea away. "How are you feeling, Phloxia? Is he better than Cyclamen? He is for me, though. I did not see a crow on his shoulder," said Abelia with a smile.

"Mother, you were better working on the kitchen," said Phloxia, seemingly not so happy.

"What is bothering you?" asked her mother.

"Mother, what if my dream is different to the dream you all have for me?" Phloxia asked as if to give a spark to her dying hopes of following her heart.

"Dreams! Dreams are all I hear about when I'm here. When you have kids, Phloxia, you will be glad to have some sleep, and dreams will be forgotten things, like an extinct species such as dinosaurs. No matter how big and powerful they are, they will be just a thing of the past," said Paulia, thinking about making another pot of tea, for all this talk was getting depressing.

"I told her already, Paulia, that dreams that do not fit in with reality are only going to make her unsatisfied, for they will never come to life. As you said, they are like dinosaurs—dream about them as you like, but can you get them back on Earth?" said Villiea.

"Dear daughters, after completing my kitchen, I have to say, dreams that come from your heart are worth giving a chance. However, then you do have to think about how they will affect others. Everyone is happy with the new kitchen, so, great. What is your dream, Phloxia?" asked her mother as Paulia went to make more tea.

"Mother, I think you probably understand now. When you were not happy living with Father, didn't you think that you would rather be with someone who you could be happy with?"

"No, I did not, Phloxia, and you shouldn't think that way either. We gave you enough freedom here, Phloxia. From now on, live like a typical D. Dron, get accepted in society, and follow the norms," said Abelia.

"What about happiness?" asked Phloxia.

"Be satisfied and happy with what you have, and as I said before, look at the people below us to become happy with what you have," her mother said as if to finish the conversation.

"I thought you had changed, Mother," said Phloxia.

"I have changed, Phloxia, and that is the reason we are having this talk. You know you cannot leave, for there is nowhere to go," said Abelia.

"I am sure Dad was dissatisfied with his own family, and, eventually, did find a way to leave," said Phloxia.

"Enough, Phloxia. Why are you bringing Dad into all this?" said Paulia.

"Yes, do what you want. Show some courage if you have any. You know as much as we do that a step outside this home means being all alone. Do you know what people with nowhere to go become? Feral cats, living in abandoned containers behind the bush," said Villiea.

"Talking about your father—he chose to leave for good, and I still remember him saying that being respectful and following the norms was his way of life, and if that leads to unhappiness, then the only way out was the one allowed by the norms. He could have chosen to live in the abandoned barn, but he did not. He followed the norms till his last breath and after. Now you decide what you would like to choose, but don't seek our permission so you can blame us tomorrow rather than your own decisions." Villiea did not want to talk about dreams, for she had learned to be happy in a difficult way.

"Time to go to bed," said their mother, looking at both Villiea and Paulia as if to ignore Phloxia.

Phloxia felt she had no value as an individual. When you are nothing, then you learn to live with what is provided to you or give up, but in both scenarios, you lose.

That was not important for Phloxia just yet, for she only wanted to sleep to numb her thinking and feelings. She was not thinking about fighting any decision, for to fight, a person needs first to find the battleground, and it was not a battleground; it was her family.

So, Phloxia—because she was bound to the habit of reading and not because she wanted to— picked up an easily accessible book, which was the one Ms Destiny had handed to her, *Hidden Desires to Destiny*, and started reading a random paragraph on a random page.

You look around and find yourself in a world that does not seem to belong to you, or you don't seem to belong to it. It is also clear that there is nothing you can do about it. The only option you seek is to give up on what you feel and accept what is readily available. You feel like a victim, for you do not have any choice but to live like a victim. For your whole life, you live like a victim, in the hope of getting sympathy from others. You become used to your sadness and suffering until you see your reflection, and your reflection denies you pity, for you are the sole reason for taking the life of your reflection. She had tried hard enough. Good night.

While reading the book, Phloxia went to sleep, and the next day, she woke up, and so passed the days, and she got married to the man of everyone's dreams.

The first couple of weeks, she felt as if it was not something she wanted, but then it became normal to have that feeling, and, eventually, she got used to living with the 'not wanting it but having to live with it' feeling, and as years passed, it became perfectly normal to see abnormal as the right option, until one day, she had a baby, and from then on, abnormal became normal, and her life became a journey that she could not wait to end.

However, when you can't wait for something, you feel as if you have to wait for a long time, and one day, in her waiting room, she had a hell of a time, for she was sick and took a day off from serving the chosen husband and the resulting baby of the relationship.

She looked into the same mirror to find her reflection, but there was nothing there. 'I have a loving husband and a beautiful kid. What else am I looking for in the mirror?' she asked herself.

"You?" a reply came.

"What do you mean"' she asked.

"You have a loving husband and a beautiful kid, but probably, in achieving all that, you lost yourself? Am I right?" a reply came.

And from then on, she could never be happy again, for the remainder of her true self shook her reality, and she felt like a leaf that survived all the big storms, rains and floods, only to fall off the tree on a sunny day after realising what it had survived and deciding to give up because it knew that it would not be able to take any more; so rather than die in a storm, it sacrificed itself voluntarily.

This is how life went on, and eventually, no one was happy with her, not her husband or her child. Who could be happy with someone so unhappy with herself?

I wish I could go back in time and choose the path my heart wanted. Then, at least my reflection would not leave me, for I would have shown the courage to follow my heart rather than being so cowardly that it gave up on me.

"Wake up, Phloxia. It is late." Phloxia opened her eyes, expecting to see the face of her husband, but, instead, there was Paulia.

"What's wrong with you? Learn to wake up early now. You

are getting married in four days."

"Oh god, wow. I am back in time," said Phloxia with much happiness.

"Back in time? No, you are not. You are getting married in four days, and there has been no change to that. Stop dreaming rubbish," said Paulia.

"Right." Phloxia was so happy to know that she still had four days. *What am I going to do, though?* And she remembered the letter given to her by Ms Martini. *I should at least go and see her, but I threw that letter in the bin, and that was the first letter to go in. Will I be able to find it? At least try, Phloxia.* She was both questioning and answering herself.

The bin was full and the letter that held the key to her future was at the bottom of it. "I wish I could go back in time," she said. "At least it is the letter, though, that is in there, and not me, as I was in my dream. I can take the rubbish out and still find the letter. At least I hope so." And Phloxia started to dig in the pile of rubbish.

"What are you doing, Phloxia? Come have some tea and clean up later," Villiea called.

"I am looking for something," said Phloxia.

"I don't know. What faulty gene is that? She is the first D. Dron to dig into the pile of rubbish," said Paulia.
"Well, it is good that she is digging into the rubbish now and will learn that playing with life is like playing with rubbish, for nothing good comes of it," said Paulia.

"I don't get it," said Villiea.

"Oh, I only wanted to seem intelligent, like we D. Drons are," said Paulia.

"It means that you should think your life is better than a bin and only fill it up with the things you want to go back and look at. Your father used to say that, so I remember," said Abelia.

"I don't know if Phloxia is confusing the bin with her life and is trying to clean it up. She seems out of her mind, as if the nonsense gene is on the job. She was talking about going back in time," said Paulia.

Villiea said that the bin was not a time-travel machine, and they all laughed.

"Let her do whatever she wants. In only four days, she will have to learn to live life like everyone else," said their mother, who was sipping on the tea.

Phloxia, on the other hand, kept digging and finally found the note. It was there, where she had left it, at the bottom, underneath a lot of things that did not matter to Phloxia.

She put it in her pocket, had a shower, got some tea, and started to wait for an opportunity to go to the address.

"Found your dream?" said Paulia jokingly.

"Found myself," replied Phloxia. "I want to go to the shops today."

"We will come with you too, Phloxia, for tomorrow, our families are coming, so it would be good to do the shopping today. What do you think, Mother?" asked Villiea.

"Sure," said their mother, who had been quiet all morning.

Phloxia was unsure how she would get to the given address and see Ms Martini with her sisters around, but it was worth taking the chance, so they all got ready to go to the shops.

Phloxia was praying to god to find a moment when she could skip off to see Ms Martini, and it is said that prayers are heard when the heart is involved. Her sisters, at one point, wanted to go to a clothing shop near the mad dogs' area. They told Phloxia to stay around and look for different things. They did not want her to go to any place that was not safe, and wanted to avoid mixing two different ideologies, for mad dogs believed in living as they liked. Aliesalbians believed in going with the flow.

So Phloxia took that opportunity and went to the address, but she could not find Ms Martini anywhere and asked a random man about her, and he did not know where she was. So she showed him the address and told him the reason for her visit anyway.

"Oh, I remember. Ms Martini talked to me about you. Yes, the ship is leaving in about a week now. I can arrange your travel. Do you have money?"

"I only have a little," she said.

"Okay, I get it. I will try to find a way to tell Ms Martini about your intentions. When will you come back?" the random man asked.

"I don't know," said Phloxia, who was uncertain of everything.

"Hmm, woman, the ship is leaving a week from now, and if you come here the day before, I will try to do something, as a favour to Ms Martini. Get as much money as you can. I will tell Ms Martini that you came here, so she will know. She would have been here to see you if the time had been fixed, but you must have some issues in life, and I can understand that. If Ms Martini's involved, the matter must be something extraordinary. She does not come here very often."

"Thank you," said Phloxia and was not sure if she should go back or not. It was like standing in the middle of a road. One way, you know, will take you safely to your end. And the other way? Only God knows where it ends. Phloxia had seen the reality that was at the end of the road if she went in the safe direction, and it made her want to go the other way. However, there was love on both sides. On one side, there was the whole family, and on the other side, there was hope for a true love of the sort we all seek no matter what is offered by family. Then someone honked a horn, for she was standing in the middle of the road and looking from side to side.

"Don't stand in the middle, woman. Choose one side and stick to it," said the man in the car.

"Did he say 'stick to it' or 'commit to it'?" she asked herself.

"Commit to it?" asked Paulia and Villiea, who had just seen their sister lost on the road full of traffic.

"What did he want you to commit to?" both sisters asked.

"I don't know," said a confused Phloxia.

"We should not have left you alone. Don't tell Mother about it."

"No, I won't. It does not matter," said Phloxia.

Villiea sensed the turmoil inside her sister and wanted to give her directions that were useful for any path, for she was her eldest sister. Hence, she said, "Phloxia, you know, mad dogs live in the abandoned barn. We call them that because they can never decide and live as they like without any rules. I only suggest that maybe you don't like our rules, but don't end up like a mad dog. At least make a decision, then build your rules, and make sure to follow them too, or as the man said, 'commit to it', dear sister. We love you."

Phloxia looked at her sister and hugged her.

They arrived home happy, and Paulia went to make tea.

"How was it?" asked Abelia.

"Great, Mum," said Villiea.

They showed their mum all the things they had bought.

"Yarrow, your uncle, brought things too, from your in-laws—some jewellery and other everyday things," their mother said.

"Hmm," said Phloxia.

"She is nervous because of the wedding, Mum," said Paulia, giving tea to everyone.

"I know. I was nervous too," her mum said, rubbing her eyebrows that were as thick and dark as the clouds of worry for Phloxia in her heart.

"Paulia dear, do the cooking, for we should go to bed early tonight. Tomorrow, everyone will be here and there might be no time to have good sleep," said their mother.

They all ate and went to their beds.

Phloxia tried to come to a decision, but this was like a choice between life and death. *I would be leaving without letting anyone know, and my family loves me. I don't know; I will have to leave it to God,* she thought. Thus, bound to her habit, she decided to do some reading from the most readily available book, *Hidden Desires to Destiny.*

When making a decision, however difficult it seems, there is always an option to choose. The easiest option is to ask yourself, 'What do I really want?' And, then, go from there.

Phloxia just put the book away, saying, 'If it was that easy to get what we really want, then we would all have what we want. There is a reason we live with unwanted things.'

With those thoughts, Phloxia slept and found herself flying in the sky like a bird with another bird. She knew they were in love. Then a storm came, and she found herself, as a woman, on an island. She called the other bird, but it was nowhere to be seen. Then, suddenly, she found herself next to the ocean, watching her man swimming and smiling.

"Come and have a swim?" he asked.

"No, I am scared," she said.

"Scared of water or scared of swimming?" he asked.

"Why don't you come here?" she asked.

"I want you to become your best self," he said.

Phloxia looked at him and kept looking at him. He was mature and kind.

"I want to meet you," she said and woke up, back in reality.

Her mother looked at her and asked her to make tea. "I want to talk to you, Phloxia, about something before your sisters are up," she said as the tea was being made.

"Dear Phloxia, we all have dreams, small or big. I had dreams too when I was your age, and I still have them, like building the kitchen the other day. However, I am talking about dreams of a man, dreams of love, and maybe true love. I had dreams, and I connected my dreams to your father when my family found him for me. After marriage, he did not seem to be the person I dreamed of, but I never questioned anything, for that is the way of life. As you know, we both were very unhappy with our choices, and I still blame my family for not researching properly. I have a right to blame them, like your sisters can blame me or your uncle, Yarrow."

"Phloxia, I already know you are unhappy. I can see your struggle. I am your mother. I don't know about your dreams, but I know they must be more potent than the ones I had, or anyone else, for they are taking your life away; if the thought of getting married is not making you happy, then life after the wedding certainly will not."

"So, Phloxia, you are free to choose anything you want, and I mean it. I will not stand with you but will not object to your choice either. I want you to decide freely so you will never blame me ever. That is all I ask."

"Your marriage date is set, so any step you take from here on, you accept responsibility for. My blessings are always with you. Yes, here, our values will be questioned, but as long as you stick to your values, it does not matter where you are; the D. Dron name will be regarded with respect."

"Come back when you find what you seek. Failures permit no turning around to the abandoned place with your own will, and as a Dron, I am sure you will get what I am saying, even though you have many faulty genes, or maybe they are the right ones. Who can decide at the end of the day?"

"Thanks, Mother," said Phloxia.

"The kitchen does look better," her mother said, smiling.

Phloxia felt relieved to have her mother's permission. The dark clouds were gone, and the sun was out. Sadness is helpful to bend mothers to a way of our liking.

Now started the race to see how Phloxia would accomplish the mission—leaving her family and going to a land she had never seen before. It was four days until her marriage was to take place, and, thus, she had three days not only to come to a decision but also to put that decision into action.

Nothing comes without paying a price. That rule has been in place for eternity. And now it remained to be seen what that price was.

During the day, all their relatives came, including Cyclamen with Cornus D. Homo Sapien, for they were related, but Cyclamen made sure to leave the crow, his godfather, behind.

Phloxia, now that she had permission from her mum, packed her bags and left to find something her heart desired. She felt she knew how the life she had on offer would unfold, so she decided it would be better to try something new and different. She reasoned that anything that happened could not be worse than what she had seen in her dream.

Phloxia, with her bags, got to the address she had been given, and she met the same man, who told her that Ms Martini would be there very soon, so she should wait for a while.

"I have come here with all my bags," she informed the random man.

"Yes, wait with the bags," the man said, "for we might have a slight problem here."

"Problem?" asked Phloxia.

"A slight problem," said the man. "This ship is mainly taking other races, the ones that are not much regarded in the land of Aliesalba but have equal rights in the land of Wellingtonia. At least that is what is said, for I have not been there."

"Does that mean I cannot go?" asked Phloxia.

"I would not know. I do not think so, but Ms Martini seems to be very caring towards you, so if I was you, then I would wait," the man said.

"Right," said Phloxia and started to wait.

And she did not have to wait for too long before Ms Martini showed up.

"Hi, Phloxia," she said, ordering some tea.

"Hi, Ms Martini. I left my home and have now been informed by this man that I might not be able to go, for this ship is only taking a different race?"

"Phloxia, that is true. You know how the world works, right? Mad dogs, as you call them, are not that different from you Aliesalbians. Their ideology is different to yours, so they are called mad dogs instead of Aliesalbians. They do walk like us and they wear casual clothes, but, otherwise, they are as Aliesalbian as you are. They talk normally and are very kind and beautiful."

"I know about mongrels. I heard stories about them from my father. He talked about how when they arrived, they tried to mix with Aliesalbians, but society did not allow it, and they were not able to integrate in great numbers, so they started living in abandoned barns. It is the same with the moggies. People call them cats, only because they have a different lifestyle and look more like cats than us Aliesalbians. They walk and talk like us, though," said Phloxia.

"Yes, mongrels share ancestors with wolves, moggies share ancestors with cats, and Aliesalbians share ancestors with apes. That is the difference. Otherwise, all look like normal humans, with two eyes, a nose, two legs, and so on."

"Except for how they think, and I heard they can still change to what they used to be," said Phloxia.

"Well, I saw two moggies the other day. One called herself domesticated and the other was feral. It is their ideology, lifestyle that is different to Aliesalbians. Otherwise, I do not see any issues myself. What you heard might just be hearsay, and if it is true, then what? It does not make any difference to me," said Ms Martini.

"The truth is, Phloxia, both moggies and mongrels think they have better futures and opportunities in the land of Wellingtonia. I heard that Wellingtonians are not as strict about ideologies and rules as here, so moggies and mongrels are allowed to live amongst them. Also, they have more work opportunities there. Here, as you know, Phloxia, people usually do not go to work, for they grow their own food and have property from ancestors, whereas in the land of Wellingtonia, things are different."

"You should know, for you are going there now, that they have royals in the land of Wellingtonia. Almost everyone else works there in some kind of capacity and it pays well too. I mean, that is the reason people, like Aliesalbians, go there, earn money, and come back, and so forth and so on."

"They do need more workers, for the land of Wellingtonia is quite advanced compared to here, as you will see when you go there, so they do need workers. Not that many Aliesalbians are interested in work, so hiring companies seek help from moggies and mongrels. And even though I see them living happily here too, who does not want to try their luck and get more than they already have?" concluded Ms Martini.

"What does that mean for me?" said Phloxia. "I thought I could go on this ship, and came here with all my belongings."

"I know, Phloxia. In this ship, all the mongrels are going. You can go as one of their partners," said Ms Martini.

"How is that possible? I am leaving my family, and if that is not enough, now I have to act as a mongrel's partner?" said Phloxia.

"There is nothing wrong with that, Phloxia. You will find that mongrels are very friendly and sophisticated. They live to be happy, and think to be happy. You could learn from them." Ms Martini put her point forward.

"But I am going there to meet the prince of my dreams," said Phloxia.

"That is right, and that is going to happen, but you have to compromise a little. This is the only way, and this is your only chance," Ms Martini said, sipping on her tea.

"I do not know; now I am confused. A mongrel? We Drons are not even allowed to talk to them," said Phloxia.

"Well, that can be arranged now," said Ms Martini and told the random man to send a mongrel there.

A good-looking man came and introduced himself as Gladiorus the mongrel. He was wearing a suit, tie and expensive shoes. He was handsome and charming.

"Hi, Gladiorus. Meet Phloxia. She wants to go to the land of Wellingtonia too and needs one of the mongrels to help her out," said Ms Martini.

"No, no, I am not decided yet," said Phloxia.

Gladiorus sat on the nearby chair, ordered some more coffee, and said, "Well, I can understand your hesitation, Phloxia. Aliesalbians never accepted us fully, and the only reason is lack of knowledge, particularly of science, I would say. I assume you know a bit of science, for I have heard about your family's faulty genes. So, apes and humans share the same ancestors, and then there is evolution, mutations, and so on and so forth. We mongrels branched off from our ancestors, the alpha wolves, due to a serious mutation. Then evolution made us more like humans. We still have the same values of honesty and loyalty, and strive to be the best in anything we do."

"Aliesalbians have difficulty accepting it. However, Wellingtonians are a thousand years ahead of Aliesalbians. It is normal there to have us around. The relationships are not that prevalent, for we are still struggling to lift our living standards due to not being fortunate enough to own ancestral assets, and most of the Wellingtonians who indulge themselves in work or were born lucky are high-class, and when it comes to relationships, as I have been observing in Aliesalbian society, it is more like a matching of economic standards than hearts. So I can understand your hesitation about becoming the partner of a mongrel," said Gladiorus, who sounded very knowledgeable.

"No, it has nothing to do with wealth," said Phloxia, feeling bad, for Gladiorus was good-looking and knew what he was talking about. "I am running from my home and think a man in Wellingtonia might be my destiny. I see him in my dreams."

"Oh, well, what if he is a mongrel?" said Gladiorus.

"No, no, he is not. At least, I think he is not," said Phloxia, trying to think.

"Well, Phloxia, we mongrels are still not that into love and go with our primitive instincts when it comes to those feelings. If you feel your love might be in the land of Wellingtonia and are happy to gamble your family, your security and everything else, then there has to be someone there, and if not, then you can live like one of us mongrels, for family, security and everything else, we do not have, but I believe we can earn it if we want to, even though I do not like to worry too much about all that stuff."

Phloxia looked at Ms Martini.

"It is your bad luck, Phloxia. I tried to do my best for you, but now this is the only option I have. You have to think about that and make your own decision," said Ms Martini.

"I just made a decision last night, and now this is another decision. What if something else goes wrong, and then I have to come up with something different again?" Phloxia was very irritated.

"This is only the start, Phloxia. If it was that easy for dreams to come true, then people would not stop dreaming or change their dreams. You are trying to create the same reality that you see in your dream, so you know you will have to face difficulties. This is the start. I don't know what kind of problems will occur on the way or even after, but are you ready to still keep moving in the direction of your dream? Because if you aren't, then you had better give up now, for once you board the ship, we both know turning back is not an option."

"Gladiorus is good-looking and smart, and if you are happy, I can arrange for you to be his partner only for the purpose of getting to Wellingtonia. What do you think?" asked Ms Martini.

"I don't know," said Phloxia. "I never thought things would be this way. I might have to go back and come back again with new thinking. Nothing is wrong with Gladiorus, but it has made me question things. What if the man I am seeking is a mongrel? Will I still love him the way I was ready to love him so far?"

"You don't have that much time, Phloxia. The schedule of the ship has changed, and it is leaving tomorrow morning. If you don't show by seven in the morning, don't bother to show up ever. I am really sorry, Phloxia. I have tried hard enough," said Ms Martini and asked Gladiorus to drop Phloxia back to her home. "Please make sure you are seen," she said, looking at Gladiorus.

Phloxia did not pay much attention and walked over to Gladiorus.

Gladiorus smiled and, following Ms Martini's instructions, dropped Phloxia off on his bike.

Ms Martini, then went back to her home thinking that *it was a good idea not to tell Phloxia about what was going on in Wellingtonia for that would only further discourage her rather than doing any help.*

"We have been looking for you, Phloxia," said the sisters. "Where have you been?"

"Oh, nowhere in particular. I just wandered around," said Phloxia.

"Hopefully, you did not wander to the abandoned shed to live like one of the cats," said Paulia.

"They are moggies, and they are good like all of us."

"Well, if moggies are good, then we could find you a mongrel instead of an Aliesalbian," said Villiea.

"What is wrong with that? Mongrels do have an interesting lifestyle," said Phloxia.

"Nothing, but you would have to live in an abandoned barn," said Villiea.

"What is wrong with that? It is their home," argued Phloxia.

"Hmm, before marriage, I might have objected, but now I don't think it makes any difference, for life becomes whatever it becomes, at the end of the day," said Villiea.

"Villiea, you are wrong. Mongrels like their own kind. So, you had no chance," said Paulia.

They both laughed.

Phloxia had one last night to choose between an Aliesalbian or a mongrel, and before tonight, the choice had been between an Aliesalbian and a Wellingtonian.

Luckily, Cornus, Darmar and Cyclamen were there doing some work.

What if I was married to Cyclamen? she asked herself. *I would be either Paulia, Villiea, or my mother, and I will become one of them in two days. However, I would not be Phloxia ever again.*

What if I choose to gamble my life away for someone I have not the slightest idea about?

I will still be Phloxia, who gave up everything for love. I will be Phloxia. I will be me.

In those thoughts, Phloxia slept.

In those thoughts, Phloxia slept and found herself with her magnet Prince who was crying in a deep dark forest and wishing for a weak genome. She asked Prince the reason for immense despair. Prince said that a deadly genome had attacked Wellingtonia's men, and I would need a weak genome to share my pain.

Phloxia told him that I am unsure about the weak genome, but I am a faulty genome, so that might work. Her dream Prince held her hands with his trembling hands and said, "One day my Father King left, Queen Mother entered into her cocoon and stayed there for days; everyone wondered and were using their intellect to deal with the never seen before a ball game. However, we noticed that the cocoon had converted into a tough shell to crack. One day, Queen Mother came out of it and ordered all married men to evacuate the civilized world and live in the wilds".

"What happened in the cocoon?" asked Phloxia

"Everyone wondered, and after reading 'hidden scientific secrets', I found out that her genome had mutated to so much an extent to convert all recessive genes made of milk and water; into super dominant genes made of cast iron. That, in turn, made her the toughest DNA to crack, and who could crack such a hard to believe genome," the prince gasped.

"It is so difficult to understand," said Phloxia

I assume you know a bit of science, for I have heard about your family's faulty genes. So, apes and humans share the same ancestors, and then there is evolution, mutations, and so on and so forth. We mongrels branched off from our ancestors, the alpha wolves, due to a serious mutation. Then evolution made us more like humans. We still have the same values of honesty and loyalty, and strive to be the best in anything we do," said Prince in her dream.

"What, I have heard this before?," said Phloxia.

"And yet, you don't understand it. My mother's genome is mutated and became the deadliest genome in the whole world."

"Hmm, such a superior genome, only a man with superpowers can crack," Phloxia said in immense sadness.

"In Wellingtonia, hardly there are proper men, Phloxia; we all have the same recessive genes."

"Where on earth we would find a man with superpowers," Prince asked Phloxia.

"Somewhere far-far away in this forest." And they walked in the dark forest, it frightened Phloxia, and she woke in the middle of the night and could not make sense of her dream, or it could be something to do with Gladiorus' talk on evolution, she thought, but one thing she was sure of was that her Prince needed help.

'and to you, I love; not to a Prince
though you are a scared Prince, the bravest, in my heart'

While Prince Deutzo and Phloxia were meeting in dreamland, In the real Wellingtonia's world, preparations were going with full force for 'The Most Eligible Bachelor of Wellingtonia'.

It was announced everywhere that a Princess with a perfect genome was required to win a Prince's heart, and to prove the potency of their genome, one would have to shoot the fish's eye using a bow and an arrow. The word never got to Aliesalba, for they did not have Royals.

The men around the abandoned lake prayed to God to give them a faulty genome rather than an all dominant genome. The nuclear reactor was ready. Mad Solo was worried that if they found another genome as deadly as the present one using a fish's eye as bait, it would take hundreds of years to produce two superpowers and to find two faulty genomes with the calibre to deal with the deadly genome was impossible. The result would be as fatal as using the nuclear bomb; Wellingtonia would never recover from it and would have to live with the consequences forever.

"But what could we do?" asked Prince Deutzo to Mad Solo, who had come to motivate the men; and rather needed motivation himself. Prince Deutzo knew that as soon as a princess wins 'The Bachelor' that would render his time up in the palace,

Wellingtonia will be ruled by women forever and men tortured. Also, now that Mad Solo gave further insight into the future of Wellingtonia, he entered into survival mode and would do anything to save his kingdom.

Thus, he asked again to Mad Solo to come up with a solution.

"We need a genome that has its flaws; a genome that is neither from Wellingtonia nor a royal. These two conditions must meet to fight your mother's genome," said Mad Solo.

"Where and how we do that?" asked Prince Deutzo, visibly saddened.

"I know where and I have faith that someone is figuring out how. So, we go and sit on the port, and wait for it to arrive." suggested Mad Solo for he knew that Magical Love was at work.

"What if she fails? Only a perfect genome can win The Bachelor designed by all dominant genome, and even if she wins, then not being a Princess will be caught by Queen Mother's Spidery eyes," Prince Deutzo argued.

"Prince Deutzo superpower is ready, and we must keep doing what we can do without predicting the future," said Mad Solo with popped up eyes.

That concluded the decision, and all men with one piercing and Mad Solo with popped up eyes, went to the port to wait for a faulty genome that did not belong to Wellingtonia and Royalty.

In Aliesalba when Phloxia woke up, the story had taken a whole new turn, but at least, for Phloxia, the fog had settled on the grass rather than on her eyes. Dreams do have an equal chance of going wrong as going right. That's why we have been calling it a gamble. However, I am sure that some dreams are worth the gamble, especially those involving love. *Also, now I know that my Prince needs help thus would do anything to help him.*

"Why would you not tell her the truth that it is not a gamble but her love is really there?" asked Magical Love, looking at Ms Destiny.

"I thought about what The God of Humanity said. The point is to see how strong the power of love is; the point is not to make them meet."

"Wow. Do you think she will show up tomorrow?" asked Magical Love.

"Oh, I am pretty sure Phloxia will, for she has started thinking actively," said Ms Destiny.

"Let's celebrate then," said Magical Love.

"I am afraid we will have to delay, for I am worried about something else," said Ms Destiny.

"There is nothing to worry about anymore; everything is set to roll." Magical Love was confident.

"I am worried about Mr Fate and The Evil of Hate. Do you think they will allow everything to happen so easily?" questioned Ms Destiny.

"Well The Evil of Hate already changed the setting of the ship so might not interfere anymore thinking Phloxia wouldn't leave now as only Mongrels are going," said Magical Love.

"Well, I hope nothing else goes wrong, and Phloxia will be here in the morning as I have... I cannot say *planned*... but as I have been thinking."

"Do you want to go and check on the D. Drons?" asked Magical Love.

"No, I will leave it to the power within, for I have shown her the ladder, and if Phloxia cannot do the climbing, then it was not meant to be, for it will only be the first ladder and there will be more to come afterwards."

"Quite depressing, it is," said Magical Love.

"Yes, let's have some drinks," said Ms Destiny.

"Really?" asked Magical Love.

"Yes, I will not be able to bear the suspense otherwise."

So they went to a nearby pub and started drinking.

As Magical Love and Ms Destiny were drinking, Phloxia was lying in her bed thinking of waking up earlier than everyone else and leaving.

The Evil of Hate was also still awake, and he was keeping an eye on everything from his chair in the air. Strangely, though, he was not worried at all, or at least, it seemed he wasn't.

Phloxia planned to leave a letter for her mum, asking for an apology for whatever happened, and then leave to the new land. What happened there would be sorted in time; for now, there was only one way out of this whole situation and that was the way she had decided to choose.

It was all so quiet. There was not a single sound or anything moving. Phloxia had never experienced a night so quiet before. It was as if the night knew that it was the last night for Phloxia, and once she left, a storm in her family was to come. So, the night was quiet in sympathy with Phloxia and was preparing itself for the storm that would start once she left.

My family will understand. Phloxia looked at her sleeping mother and sisters, and she did not know how to react; only tears started to run down her face. *Why does it have to come to facing a situation that involves having to choose between family and love? Why can love only happen when there is a challenge involved? Love must be created by evil to amuse itself, for God would not play with hearts.* Phloxia answered her own questions. *Anyhow, I will make sure I succeed.*

Phloxia wiped her tears and got ready to leave.

At about three in the morning, she was about to leave, but, strangely, a hailstorm came that no one expected. That kind of storm had never come before. Phloxia still gathered her courage and was about to leave, but her mother called her from behind. "Phloxia, are you getting the clothes from the clothesline? Don't worry about it, my child. It is hailing. Come back in." That left Phloxia with no choice. Love for her mother, more than the fear of getting caught, stopped her.

The storm got worse and worse, and all night, the winds were strong, as if trying to turn destinies around, and the hail was big enough to kill anyone who showed courage and didn't follow the order given by the winds.

In the morning, at about eight, the severe weather died down, and happiness started to dance around. Everyone was happy, except Phloxia. *But what could I have done? The weather stopped me, or evil—one of those,* she thought. *I was crying and challenging evil, and it seems that it accepted the challenge. But I am being silly. Why would anyone care about me leaving or staying? Unless it was someone from my family, but no one in my family is capable of causing supernatural events.*

What will I do now? I have to wait for another night, for even if the ship has left today, there will be another one. I will live at the port forever if necessary. In a way, it is good I did not get to board this one; if anyone had seen me leaving with a mongrel to the land of Wellingtonia, it would be a lifelong insult for my family. It will be better to go alone.

"Wake up, wake up," Ms Destiny said to Magical Love.
"What?" asked Magical, still high on the drinks from the night before.
"Our hopes have been wiped out by your dear friends."

"What do you mean?"

"The Evil of Hate has played his last card and stopped Phloxia from running away by creating a hailstorm." Ms Destiny was angry.

"Oh, a hailstorm? I missed that part," said Magical Love, looking outside. "Why are you worried, though? Remember what you said last night? Oh, you would not, for you got drunk afterwards. You said it was the first ladder, and Phloxia has to go up herself—something like that."

"Yes, I did, but I did not know then that the ladder would be wiped out by your friends. She at least needs a ladder; she can't climb the air. I have to create another set-up, and this time, one so confusing that, leaving The Evil of Hate aside, no one will understand what is going on. The ladder will not be put up until she is ready to take her first step. The Evil of Hate has thrown out a challenge to me, and I accept it.'

"What are you going to do? Would I understand?" asked Magical Love.

"Tell me if you do," said Ms Destiny and smiled.

The Evil of Hate saw events from his high chair and sensed the developing urgency of the situation. He called in Mr Fate from the land of Wellingtonia, and he came in no time, for he had extra-terrestrial powers.

As soon as Mr Fate got there, he started to give updates on Deutzo Hydrang's life for a lot was going there "I do not have words to describe the scenario that is unfolding in Wellingtonia," he said.

"Good, good, I would hear about your scenario later. But that is not what I have called you in for. There is something else going on. Phloxia is getting married in two days."

"You should be happy then, my friend," said Mr Fate, who

was wearing glasses that didn't allow others to know what he was looking at.

"Take those things off your eyes and look around. Do you see all the hail damage created by the storm? I did it to stop her from doing anything crazy to avoid her wedding. However, Destiny has accepted the challenge and will try to stop her wedding. I want you to keep an eye on Ms Destiny 24/7, even if your eyes are strained. Make sure she doesn't do anything to stop the wedding," said The Evil of Hate.

"I can do that," said Mr Fate. "But should we not keep an eye on Phloxia so she does not run away?"

"She will not go anywhere anymore, for she is too emotional, and that is making her slow to take any action. Also, she is confused within. If it was not for Ms Destiny, she would not even consider leaving."

"I get you. I will make sure that Ms Destiny does not do anything that does any damage to the damage that you did to stop the damage of us losing the battle before it has even started," said Mr Fate.

"Go, do your job. It is time for me to rest my eyes, for I have been keeping an eye on this whole situation all by myself, but I have to say, it was worth it. We are winning." The Evil of Hate was happy.

"We are winners. And the losers are now being watched closely by a winner to make sure the tables do not turn," said Mr Fate.

"Yes, go now," said The Evil of Hate.

"Yes, a winner is leaving," said Mr Fate.

Ms Destiny asked Magical Love to come with her to a cafe and sit with her as she planned something while having coffee.

"My brain usually works after having one or two coffees,"

she told Magical Love.

"I know you are very sensitive to not having caffeine." Magical Love looked at her with love.

"Two coffees, please?" she asked.

Two coffees arrived, and they started drinking, while Mr Fate was having a cup of tea and closely watching them from another table.

"The coffee is tasty," said Ms Destiny.

"Indeed," replied Magical Love.

Ms Destiny kept talking, and Magical Love kept listening.

While they were talking, Phloxia was getting ready for the dance and party that was to continue for the next two days. She was trying to stay away from everyone and was trying to distract herself from reality.

Everyone was out to dance. Abelia was still making sure all the jewellery was in the safe, and as she was about to go out, Yarrow came in, and there came another storm with him. They both suddenly started feeling sorry for Phloxia. Then Yarrow Dron left, and Abelia sat there as if to think of something. However, in no time, he came back with another storm, but this storm brought hail with it, not like the hail from the morning, but like hail that showered happiness all over the D. Dron house, and so they both were not sad anymore. Rather, they started talking about how the times were changing.

"Phloxia, you are very lucky," said her mother, who had gone to see her first thing after the two storms, for she could feel the pain of her daughter, and now that she knew the real story, she wanted to make her happy.

"If I was you, I would be happy. The times are changing, and all that matters is love. That is what you wanted, so make sure to love your husband. He is good; everyone knows him. Your uncle knows him; that is the reason he agreed to it. He is a real gem. I know the early morning storm disappointed you, but that was an event, a warning, to stop you from doing what you were to do."

"I know that you were planning to leave. I know I gave you permission to, but it would have brought shame to the whole family. Maybe I would blame myself more than you, but now everything is as it was supposed to be. Everyone is happy. I know you have dreams and wishes, but all you wanted was to marry someone you love. So, make sure to love the one your destiny has chosen for you."

"What happened, Mother? What did Uncle bring when he stormed into your room?" asked Phloxia.

"Dear Phloxia." Her mother smiled. "You should have told us about it earlier."

"What, Mother? There are so many things. Which part are you talking about?" asked Phloxia.

But before her mother could answer, the dance started, and her sisters took her outside, where the wedding songs were playing.

Phloxia was made to dance to a song.

The next morning, everyone got ready, and so did Phloxia. *It seems so unreal,* she thought. But it was not.

She was getting married, and she was expecting her husband. But then she saw Gladiorus. She was getting married to Gladiorus? "How?" she asked him.

"'That, I will tell you about later, but we have to leave," he said.

So as soon as they got married, everyone hugged her and let her go happily.

"Come back in six months," her mum said.

"Six months?"

But before anyone could answer, she was on the way to the

port and was put straight on the ship, while Ms Destiny was having coffee with Magical Love again, for she could not think without coffee, and Mr Fate was watching them as instructed and had not slept all night.

"How did that happen?" Phloxia asked Gladiorus.

"Well, it all happened when I took you back to your house, and Ms Martini told me to be visible so others could see me, remember?"

"I do, but I thought that she was joking," said Phloxia.

"Well, she wasn't, so I made sure to make quite a noise so people would see me, and it got back to your intended in-laws, eventually. At first, they did not object, but then they considered the morning storm as a warning. Thus, they gave a letter to your uncle."

"Yes, I remember he stormed in," said Phloxia.

"Yes, and they told him what people saw. Your uncle knows me, and we are good friends, for I have introduced him to one of the moggies, and they are currently friends for he could not connect to her otherwise."

"My uncle?"

"Yes, Your Uncle Yarrow. There is a reason he is single. He has a tough genome to crack. Anyhow, he came to me and asked me if that was the truth, and I said yes. He asked me if I wanted to marry you. Now, I had no objection, for I am single, and you are all right too. The times are changing these days. We might have a different ideology and look a little different, but I am sure you liked me the other day. Also, I knew that you wanted to go to the land of Wellingtonia, so I thought you would be fine with it. However, the important reason was your wedding. What would everyone think if it was cancelled?" said Gladiorus.

"That is how it happened. You owe Ms Martini a favour,

though. It would not have been possible without her help."

"Oh, my god. But, Gladiorus, you don't know anything else. I need to tell you something."

"I wanted to go to the land of Wellingtonia for different reasons. You know actually, don't you?"

"That's all right. You can tell me later, for we are going to be together for a long time. Come and enjoy the journey to the land of Wellingtonia." Gladiorus was very excited, for he was to start a whole new life.

Phloxia was not sure whether to be happy or sad. She was just confused, and so was Magical Love as he sat looking at Ms Destiny drinking coffee after coffee.

"Are you all right, Ms Destiny?" asked Magical Love. "I thought we were here to make a plan for Phloxia? You have accepted the challenge but are doing nothing, though."

"I am going to tell you something, Magical Love. One, I arrange everything before accepting a challenge. Two, I am not you. I do not wait for fate or destiny to make things happen. I am destiny, and I happen when someone wants me badly enough. Time to get the second ladder ready." And Ms Destiny winked and smiled.

It was the fastest ship on the water, and in no time, Phloxia could see the land of Wellingtonia in the distance. She was trying to make sense of what had just happened and was trying to imagine how her life could unravel in the land of Wellingtonia. *Is there still a chance to meet the man I dream of?* She thought, looking at Gladiorus the Mongrel.

On the other hand, The Evil of Hate was getting angry at Mr Fate.

"So, you did not follow my instructions?" asked The Evil of Hate.

"I did, but Ms Destiny was clever to blind us all and play her game in the dark without bringing anything to light until after it was too late," Mr Fate said in her defence.

"I know, I know. Give me updates on Wellingtonia? As you were very enthusiastic before," said The Evil of Hate.

"As you know after Mad Solo's visit to Queen Mother since then men are loose in the wild and women stay at home," said Mr Fate thinking.

"Hmm, exciting development, Such a cruel treatment of men without my involvement. I must praise the Queen Mother, and let's see how we can add salt to the misery."

Thereon everyone focused on Wellingtonia.

As Mad Solo had instructed, men from around the lake were waiting at the port for a woman containing a defective genome. As soon as Phloxia and Gladiorus got to the port, the men on the port yelled, 'found the one, found the one.' Phloxia and Gladiorus were bewildered and could not understand anything. Then Mad Solo came out of the crowd and explained to them the whole situation in brief and asked Phloxia to become the princess and shot the fish eye with a bow and an arrow.

"I have never seen a bow, an arrow, a fish," said Phloxia

"At least take a chance," begged Mad Solo with his popped up eyes. "The chances are remote that you would win; however, if you did win by chance, then that only means that another defective genome is on his way, for a person who has never seen a fish can only win with extra-terrestrial help," Mad Solo put his point forward.

Phloxia agreed, for he recently had a dream where his magnet Prince had explained the similar situation to him. Gladiorus was lost in all this but decided to go with the flow and take a chance for Mad Solo was a mongrel as him. On the way, they stopped to get clothes for Phloxia to make her look like a princess. They also bought a packet of popcorns, each of them and two eye patches. Gladiorus asked the reason and was told that he would know soon and gave him the same accessories.

On the way to the event location, Phloxia looked up and said, "Gracious God help me," and Magical Love and Ms. Destiny heard it.

"Hmm, we are so close to winning, only if Phloxia could shoot the fish's eye," said, Magical Love.

"How on earth one can knock the eye out of the rotating fish, though, unless you give the subject a magical potion?" Ms. Destiny was serious.

"Magical potion has the potency to make someone high but not make them shoot eyes, the arrow is for that, but I can't make an arrow drink the magical shake. I wish though if an arrow has eyes, then certainty taking an eye for an eye, was a possibility," Magical Love was hopeful.

"I have a eureka moment. Why don't you become eyes for the arrow?" asked Ms. Destiny.

"How so?" asked Magical Love. How could he become eyes for the arrow?

"Well, all you have to do is that as soon as the arrow leaves the bow, you get hold of it and then once it is in your possession, straight-up hit in the eye of the fish. It does not matter where is the eye is located," suggested Ms. Destiny.

"Oh, so are you suggesting an arrow flying anywhere physically without any explanation from the laws of physics?" asked Magical Love.

"Well, to save the men of Wellingtonia from lethal biology, we must play with physics or the lethal set-up designed by the most potent genome could never let the faulty genome win," Ms. Destiny put her point forward.

"Would not people see me and beat the light out of me?" asked Magical Love.

"Wear the invisible cloak, common sense."

"Would not it seem odd?" asked Magical Love.

"Well, the whole population of Wellingtonia, taking over the streets with only one earring in forced piercing isn't that odd?" Ms. Destiny put her point forward.

"Hmm, I have to do it for the success of our subject," Magical Love agreed.

"Also, remember…"

"What?" asked Magical Love.

"Do you see how other princesses are here too, to knock the eye of poor fish out in a matter of seconds?"

"Yes, so?" asked Magical Love.

"Make sure to change the course of their arrows, so their arrows don't hit the right target, or the subject might have to fight for the chemistry with Prince Deutzo Hydrang." Ms. Destiny was not leaving anything to chance.

"Did you notice Ms. Destiny how we have been talking in a coded language? I had never experienced this before."

"And you never will. It only happens in Wellingtonia, for women's genome is highly coded here and affects everyone in the vicinity. Try not to come in contact with any coded women when on a mission knocking fish's eye's out, or it does not matter you are unseen. Your codes will be cracked in minutes and leave you as lost love with popped eyes. Then you will have to quarantine for one year like Mad Solo, who recovered for he was a scientist, but for you, chances are remote."

"Hmm," said Magical Love, thinking seriously about the

ramifications of all dominant genome on the world, once Wellingtonia is taken over completely. That thought scares him, and he decided to make the operation 'Changing the direction of arrows' successful. So, he took the invisible cloak and went to the location of 'The Bachelor of Wellingtonia' with Ms. Destiny.

As soon as Phloxia arrived at the event, she was introduced as the Princess Phloxia of Aliesalba by Gladiorus, who was acting as her assistant. However, Phloxia realised that her imperfect genome showed sensitivity to light because of nervousness. Every time she tried to look around, her eyes would close in fear of arrows. Her nonsense gene sought impressions that would question her suitability as a candidate to hold the bow and render it impossible for her to compete in the event. She wished for God to make it the darkest day, so no one would know where her arrows went, and in this confusion, she might physically pierce the fish's eyes with her hands and keep the bow at bay.

"Oh, strange Phloxia, suddenly everything is gone so dark as if a big storm is to come," said Gladiorus looking at the sky.

"God heard me," thought Phloxia.

After the registration, Phloxia was ready to compete with the other princesses.

There were sitting men from around the lake in public, and leading them was Mad Solo. All men with one earring in their ears, all kinds of earrings, and each of them holding a packet of popcorn in their hand. Gladiorus was shocked to see such a display of tortured men in the hands of the killer genome but still wondered why they were holding a bag of unpopped popcorn. Still, that secret was disclosed in no time when perfect genomes came from another side with all dominant genome leading them, most of them wearing one earring, and as soon as they came in the vicinity of tortured men, popcorns started to pop. Eventually, all popcorns were popped, and men began to eat them one by one, and 'The Bachelor Season of Wellingtonia' started successfully.

Gladiorus and Phloxia were confused about how the popcorns popped.

"Oh, yeah, you don't know this part; when killer genome is around, it must pop something out of Wellingtonia's men. Thus, we brought popcorns to save our eyes, not eat them. Mad Solo told them, pointing at his eyes.

"Makes sense now," said Gladiorus.

The Queen Mother greeted and honoured all the participants at the appropriate time and announced that her son Prince Deutzo Hydrang would enter the hall. Amidst the sounds of bugles, drums and melodious music, Prince Deutzo entered the bachelor hall. As soon he entered, all eyes turned toward him.

Everyone seriously listened to the instruction given by the Queen Mother, the lethal genome.

"Honourable princesses, I hope you can see a fish hanging from a revolving wheel fixed at the top of a pillar with your unpopped eyes. The reflection of the fish is seen in a wide pan full of oil, placed at the bottom of the pillar."

"The Princess, who hits the fish's eye while looking at the reflection, shall win the hand of my son, the bachelor Prince Deutzo Hydrang, who is ready to be pierced and join one earring wearing men to live around the abandoned lake." A bow and a quiver full of thirteen arrows were placed on the competitors' stage.

The event began, and only three princesses came forward, including Phloxia, who thanked God for dark clouds again, for otherwise, she would never be able to face the arrows in light.

The ones who had placed bets on their love story were to

watch the live performance of Princess Phloxia D. Dron—everyone such as the Evil of Hate, Mr. Fate, Magical Love and Ms. Destiny were there with eyes undercover. It was good that Phloxia was unaware that there were people visible to an open eye and the ones not visible to a visible eye were there.

Otherwise, she could never be able to perform. The clouds had started to rumble, and there was lightning only to warn of upcoming arrows.

The rain of the arrows has not started yet, but the first princess had picked the bow. Then as the rain of arrows started, everyone covered their eyes. Magical Love wrapped himself in an invisible cloak, ready to change the course of upcoming arrows. One by one, each arrow of princess number one, was to pop the eye out of the fish. Thirteen-times Magical Love had to direct them to any eye that had dared to stay open and question the laws of physics. Princess number one's eyes popped out in shock of seeing her arrows dominating over her dominant genome. The same was repeated with princess number two.

And no one watched this godly act only from fear of getting their eyes popped. Men with one pierced ear had their eyes hidden behind the eye covers they purchased earlier and also the popcorn packets. The most lethal genome itself had to hide behind the royal chair, for almost all arrows were directed toward her spidery eyes after course correction by Magical Love unless any other daring looks needed to be popped. Magical Love was flying around, arrows in hands under the invisible cloak.

Then came Princess Phloxia D Dron, who was afraid the first time, faced the crowd, and her eyes were already popped out with fear. So Magical Love threw the invisible cloak away, for no eye could dare to face the arrow's rain; that was to come from the bow held by a faulty genome, and all eyes were under some sort of cover.

Phloxia tried to look at Gladiorus to get some courage, but his eyes were undercover.

Then she tried to look at Deutzo Hydrang, but he was under cover of the royal chair, for who does not like intact eyes. Then she looked around, and everyone was either undercover or underground with no visible eyes to her popped eyes. That made her fearless to start the rain of the arrows, but her popped eyes suddenly began to flutter, thanks to Mr. Fate trying to defeat her.

Her brain could not process all the godly acts around her and left her left side, and eventually her right side too. And she had no idea what the task was and started looking at the bow in her hand with fluttering and popped up eyes.

It could not be happening, she thought, but how would she use the bow when her brain totally refused to be on either side. She wanted to pick up an arrow and pierce the fish's eye with her hands, but the reaction of two godly powers actions was her inability to perform any task.

Help me, God, she asked, looking up and Magical Love was standing next to her waiting for an arrow, but when he received the distress signal from the subject, he realised the interference by Fate. Thus, Magical Love picked up the arrow from the quivers, popped the fish's eye, and left the arrow inside as proof that Phloxia's bow had invaded the eye. And that was only possible due to all eyes being undercover all the time.

Then a strong gush of wind hit Phloxia. So as everyone and one by one all eyes started to open. Everyone saw poor fish's invaded eye, and the bow was in Phloxia's hand, which rendered her the winner.

Prince Deutzo looked at Phloxia, which reminded him of the

Princess he had seen in his dreams, and the same happened for Phloxia. They kept looking into each other's eyes, no matter popped or not, for they only had eyes for each other.

The Queen Mother announced the winner finally, and then Phloxia finally realised she had won. As people started leaving due to the harsh weather, everyone's mouth was opened in awe, due to a miraculous win of such an unexceptional winner, whose arrow hit the fish's eye and no one could see.

That rendered the bachelor successful and now started the real battle how to save Prince Deutzo from the deadly eyes of his all dominant mother to leave him out of the palace and also how to bring all the men of Wellingtonia back home.

The Queen Mother decided to gather everyone on high tea to have a task force ready to arrange Deutzo's wedding, piercing and departure all at the same time.

Thus, with the help of all women in making tea, it was served out in the two-acre yard. The Queen Mother took the main seat.

The Queen Mother then looked at the Gladiorus, acting as Phloxia's assistant and a messenger from Aliesalba. She said that as it was seen that Princess Phloxia had won, amid all closed eyes, and to everyone's amazement, had popped the eye out of the fish, with her popped and fluttering eyes. "Such an act has rendered the bachelor to go down in the history book. From here on, ever again, the performance of this calibre, a calibre even more fatal than my shotgun, will not be repeated for ages to come. We were lucky to be presented during the performance, even though our peepers were undercover. However, now it is time for our Prince Deutzo Hydrang to become her husband and thus, leave the mansion to leave us all pure genome containers."

"Thus, messenger Gladiorus, I would like to you prepare your men lot that have arrived here from Aliesalba to go back to your prime land where a pure genome of an unbeatable calibre was born. I invite all royals of Aliesalba to join us here for the wedding. Once they are happy with the arrangement done in Wellingtonia of their daughter's future with one earring on, then we arrange the wedding."

Phloxia looked at Gladiorus, and Gladiorus looked at Phloxia, thinking where and how would they arrange the royals of Aliesalba. However, Prince Deutzo Hydrang looked at both of them, assuring them that Mad Solo would come up with a solution.

Prince Deutzo Hydrang asked his mother to show them all around Wellingtonia before the departure. The Queen Mother showed no objection, for after the wedding Prince Deutzo was to leave the mansion at once to go to the wild so he should take this time to mingle with his to be a wife and her assistant.

Straight away Phloxia, Gladiorus, and Prince Deutzo went to meet Mad Solo and ask him about the next step. Prince Deutzo told him that Phloxia was from a defective genome family and not a perfect genome royal.

Mad Solo suggested bringing her family and playing as royals, for another faulty genome must show up very soon. The nuclear reactor showed signs that the superpower was ready by going active with fire coming out through the chimney instead of pure smoke at times.

Phloxia showed her concerns about whether the Queen Mother would ever change, but Mad Solo told her to play along as help is on the way with his bat to beat the killer genome.
Thus, Phloxia, with Mad Solo's assurance, went back and her family was shocked to see her return so soon.

Her mother only said they tolerated her for twenty years, give and take one, and Wellingtonia could not have her for even one week?

Phloxia explained everything to Uncle Yarrow, who rejected her story at first, but Gladiorus confirmed. Thus, Yarrow believed and decided to take a leap of faith and go along with the flow only for men lot.

Phloxia then explained everything to Abelia, Paulia and Villiea and told them the need for a defective genome in Wellingtonia. Thus, they took off to Wellingtonia, where the Queen Mother received them as royals.

A bizarre thing happened; for the first time in her life since coming out of the cocoon, the Queen Mother took her goggles off and looked at Yarrow Dron and kept looking. However, once she realised that she was looking at Yarrow Dron and everyone was looking at her, she put her goggles back on.

From his hiding, Mad Solo noticed that, so did Prince Deutzo and Phloxia. It was the first time since King Father had left the Queen Mother that she ever looked at a man with such an interest.

The family union went alright with no significant disturbance for enchanting. Yarrow Dron did most of the work to run the event smoothly. The royal wedding certainly was a big event; however, the main event was piercing Prince Deutzo Hydrang and letting him loose in the wild with other men. Phloxia did not want to do that. Still, she had no choice, for Prince Deutzo Hydrang wanted her to listen to the Queen Mother.

Thus after the emotional ear piercing of Prince Deutzo, the earrings were exchanged, and he was taken to the abandoned lake by Yarrow Dron to give him company. However, as soon as Yarrow crossed the nuclear reactor, it started showing signs of activity by producing continuous fire then the smoke coming out of it earlier. That was a call of action for Mad Solo, and he asked Yarrow Dron if he had defective genes.

Yarrow Dron said he was unsure if he had defective genes, but D. Drons have faulty genes, so he might as well.

"Hmm, then you must have a defective genome, same as the one that is needed to take the superpower to remove the invisible force from around the deadly genome. The force that is keeping her off from showing any sign of weakness."

"Have you ever been bitten by a bat? I am only curious because I wonder how D. Drons got so many defective genomes. In my research, it was evident that bats have defective genes, for they stay away at night whereas everyone else sleeps."

"Yes, indirectly, maybe for once my mother beat me with a bat," said Yarrow, thinking.

"Perfect," said Mad Solo.

"There is superpower in there; in this nuclear reactor," Mad Solo looks at Yarrow Dron and Prince Deutzo, "It is wanting to come out since Yarrow has bestowed the lake."

"Prince Deutzo, would you please ask your in-laws to take superpower to the killer genome so men can go back to their homes."

Prince Deutzo explained everything to visibly upset Yarrow Dron.

"What is the superpower?" asked Yarrow Dron, and everyone started looking at each other for, no one knew the answer, not even Mad Solo. Yarrow Dron thus decided to take risks for his niece's happiness. He stood in front of the nuclear reactor and asked superpower to come out. After a while, a letter came out. Yarrow Dron looked at the letter and knew what he had to do.

He returned to the palace, and the rest of the men followed, thinking he was the saviour. Phloxia was still standing at the gate crying and looking toward the lake, waiting for a miracle to happen and bring Prince Deutzo back home. The Queen Mother was saddened a little for her son, and her love interest had left but still was full of strength and no sign of visible weakness.

Yarrow Dron went straight to the Queen Mother, who had stood up seeing Yarrow. Yarrow Dron held her hand and said, "Oh dear, I love you, give me your strengths and take my weaknesses, fill the world with equality and humanity."

That made the Queen Mother cry, and 'The Deadly Force' left her, and the superpower was the words of love. The Queen Mother changed from killer genome to the kind Queen Mother, for there was no need of a killer genome, for she was filled with love. Yarrow Dron, who was stag too, had liked Queen Mother too, and they both got married.

Queen Mother found out that neither Phloxia nor Yarrow Dron were royals.

Still, she said what a royal could not do, a defective genome's stag did and did not matter the royalty only love matters. All men were allowed to return to their homes.

Phloxia and Deutzo Hydrang fell in love more and more each passing day and lived happily ever after.

Mad Solo's eyes were healed eventually.

As love won, so did the God of Humanity.